Five Go Off To Camp

Enid Blyton

THE FAMOUS FIVE

Five Go Off To Camp

Hodder
Children's
Books

A division of Hachette Children's Books

Enid Blyton ® Famous Five ® Copyright © Chorion Rights Ltd
All rights reserved
'Foreword' copyright Sophie Smallwood 2010

First published in Great Britain in 1947 by Hodder and Stoughton

This revised edition first published in 2010 by Hodder Children's Books

With thanks to Rachel Elliot

The right of Enid Blyton to be identified as the Author of
the Work has been asserted by her in accordance with the
Copyright, Designs and Patents Act 1988.

2

A Catalogue record for this book is available from the British Library

ISBN 978 0 340 93165 3

Typeset by Avon DataSet Ltd, Bidford-on-Avon, Warwickshire

P.   plc

The pap   n's Books
are nat   tainable
forest   mental

Contents

1 Holiday time

'Two sturdy tents, four groundsheets, four sleeping bags – hey, what about Timmy? Isn't he going to have a sleeping bag too?' said Dick, with a grin.

The other three children laughed, and Timmy, the dog, thumped his tail hard on the ground.

'Look at him,' said George. 'He's laughing, too! He's got his mouth stretched wide open.'

They all looked at Timmy. He really did look as if a wide grin stretched his hairy mouth from side to side.

'He's a darling,' said Anne, hugging him. 'Best dog in the world, aren't you, Timmy?'

'Woof!' said Timmy, agreeing. He gave Anne a wet lick on her nose.

The four children – Julian, tall and strong for his age, Dick, George and Anne – were busy planning a camping holiday. George was a girl, not a boy, but she'd never answer to her real name, Georgina. With her freckled face and short, curly hair she really did look more like a boy than a girl.

'It's absolutely brilliant, being allowed to go on a camping holiday all by ourselves,' said Dick. 'I never thought our parents would allow it, after the amazing adventure we had last summer, when we went off in caravans.'

'Well – we won't be *completely* all by ourselves,' said Anne. 'Don't forget we've got Mr Luffy to keep an eye on us. He'll be camping nearby.'

'Old Luffy!' said Dick, with a laugh. 'He won't know if we're there or not. As long as he can study his precious moorland insects, he won't bother about us.'

'Well, if he hadn't been going to camp, too, we wouldn't have been allowed to go,' said Anne. 'I heard Dad say so.'

Mr Luffy was a teacher at the boys' boarding school, an elderly, dreamy man with a passion for studying all kinds of insect-life. Anne avoided him when he carried around boxes of insect specimens, because sometimes they escaped and came crawling out. The boys liked him and thought him fun, but the idea of Mr Luffy keeping an eye on them struck them as very funny.

'It's more likely we'll have to keep an eye on *him*,' said Julian. 'He's the sort of man whose tent will always be falling down on top of him, or he'll run out of water, or sit down on his bag of eggs. Mr Luffy seems to live in the world of insects, not in our world!'

'Well, he can go and live in the world of insects if he likes, as long as he doesn't interfere with us,' said George, who hated interfering people. 'This sounds as if it'll be a brilliant holiday – living in tents on the high moors, away from everybody, doing exactly what we like, when we like and how we like.'

'Woof!' said Timmy, thumping his tail again.

'That means he's going to do as *he* likes, too,' said Anne. 'You're going to chase hundreds of rabbits, aren't you, Timmy, and bark madly at anyone who dares to come within two miles of us!'

'Be quiet a minute, Anne!' said Dick, picking up his list again. 'We have to check down our list and find out if we've got every single thing we want. Where did I get to – oh, four sleeping bags.'

'Yes, and you wanted to know if Timmy was to

have one,' said Anne, with a giggle.

'Of course he won't,' said George. 'He'll sleep where he always does – won't you, Timmy? On my feet.'

'Couldn't we get him just a *small* sleeping bag?' asked Anne. 'He'd look sweet with his head poking out of the top.'

'Timmy hates looking sweet,' said George. 'Go on, Dick. I'll tie my hanky round Anne's mouth if she interrupts again.'

Dick went on down his list. It was a very interesting one. Things like cooking stoves, canvas buckets, enamel plates and drinking cups were on it and each item seemed to need a lot of discussion. The four children enjoyed themselves very much.

'It's almost as much fun planning a holiday like this as having it,' said Dick. 'Well – I don't think we've forgotten a thing, have we?'

'No. We've probably thought of too much!' said Julian. 'Mr Luffy says he'll take all our things on the trailer behind his car, so we'll be all right. I wouldn't like to carry them ourselves!'

'Oh, I wish next week would come!' said Anne. 'Why is it that the time seems so long when you're waiting for something nice to happen, and so short when something nice *is* happening?'

'Yes, it's the wrong way around, isn't it?' said Dick, with a grin. 'Anyone got the map? I'd like to take another look at the spot where we're going.'

Julian produced a map from his pocket. He opened it and the four children sprawled around it. The map showed a vast and lonely stretch of moorland, with very few houses indeed.

'Just a few small farms, that's all,' said Julian pointing to one or two. 'They can't get much of a living out of such poor land, though. See, that's about the place where we're going – just there – and on the opposite slope is a small farm where we'll get milk, eggs and butter when we need them. Luffy's been there before. He says it's a small farm, but really useful to campers.'

'These moors are very high, aren't they?' said George. 'I guess they'll be freezing cold in the winter.'

'They are,' said Julian. 'And they may be windy and cold in the summer, too, so Luffy says we'd better take jumpers and things. He says in the winter they're covered with snow for months. The sheep have to be dug out when they get lost.'

Dick's finger followed a small winding road that made its way over the wild stretch of moorland.

'That's the road we go,' he said. 'And I suppose we break off here, look, where a cart-track is shown. That must go to the farm. We'll have to carry our stuff from wherever Luffy parks his car, and take it to our camping place.'

'Not too near Luffy, I hope,' said George.

'Oh, no. He's agreed to keep an eye on us, but he'll forget all about us once he's settled down in his own tent,' said Julian. 'He will, really. Two boys I know once went out in his car with him for a day's run, and he came back without them in the evening. He'd forgotten he had them with him, and had left them wandering somewhere miles and miles away.'

'Good old Mr Luffy,' said Dick. 'That's the sort of grown-up we want! He won't come springing up to ask if we've cleaned our teeth or if we've got our warm jumpers on!'

The others laughed, and Timmy stretched his doggy mouth into a grin again. His tongue hung out happily. It was good to have all four of his friends with him again, and to hear them planning a holiday. Timmy went to school with George and Anne in term time, and he missed the two boys very much. But he belonged to George, and wouldn't dream of leaving her. It was a good thing that George's school allowed pets, or George would certainly not have gone!

Julian folded up the map again.

'I hope all the things we've ordered will come in time,' he said. 'We've got about six days to wait. I'd better keep on reminding Luffy that we're going with him, or he's quite likely to start without us!'

It was difficult to have to wait so long now that everything was planned. Parcels came from various shops and were eagerly opened. The sleeping bags were good.

'Wonderful!' said Anne.

'Brilliant!' said George, crawling into hers. 'Look! I can lace it up at the neck – and it's got a hood thing to come right over my head. It's really warm! I won't mind the coldest night if I'm sleeping in this. Let's sleep in them tonight.'

'What? In our bedrooms?' said Anne.

'Yes. Why not? Just to get used to them,' said George, who felt that a sleeping bag was a hundred times better than an ordinary bed.

So that night all four slept on the floor of their bedrooms in their sleeping bags, and found them very comfortable and as warm as toast.

'The only thing is, Timmy kept wanting to come right inside mine,' said George, 'and honestly there isn't enough room. Besides, he'd be cooked.'

'Well, he seemed to spend half the night on my tummy,' grumbled Julian. 'I'll keep the bedroom door shut if Timmy's going to spend the night flopping on everyone's bag in turn.'

'I don't mind the flopping, so much as the terrible habit he's got of turning himself around and around and around before he flops down,' complained Dick. 'He did that on me last night. Silly habit.'

'He can't help it,' said George at once. 'It's a habit that wild dogs had centuries and centuries ago – they slept in reeds and rushes, and they got into the way of turning themselves around and around in them, to trample them down and make themselves a good sleeping place. And our dogs go on turning themselves around now, before they go to sleep, even though there aren't any rushes to trample down.'

'I wish Timmy would forget his doggy ancestors

were wild dogs with rushy beds, and just remember he's a nice tame dog with a basket of his own,' said Dick. 'You should see my stomach today! It's all printed over with his paw marks.'

'Fibber!' said Anne. 'You do exaggerate, Dick. Oh, I wish Tuesday would come. I'm tired of waiting.'

'It'll come all right,' said Julian.

And so it did, of course. It dawned bright and sunny, with a sky that was a deep blue, flecked with tiny white clouds.

'Good-weather clouds,' said Julian, pleased. 'Now let's hope Mr Luffy has remembered it's today we're starting off. He's due here at ten o'clock. We're taking sandwiches for everyone. Mum thought we'd better, in case Luffy forgot his. If he's remembered them it won't matter, because we're sure to be able to eat them ourselves. And there's always Timmy to finish things up!'

Timmy was as excited as the four children. He always knew when something nice was going to happen. His tail was wagging the whole time, his tongue hung out, and he panted as if he'd been running a race. He kept getting under everyone's feet, but nobody minded.

Mr Luffy arrived half an hour late, just when everyone was beginning to think he'd forgotten to come. He was at the wheel of his big old car, smiling. All the children knew him quite well, because he lived not far away and was friendly with their parents.

'Hello, hello!' he cried. 'All ready, I see! Good! Pile the things on the trailer, will you? Mine are there too but there's plenty of room. I've got sandwiches for everyone, by the way. My wife said I'd better bring plenty.'

'We'll have a feast today then,' said Dick, helping to carry out the folded-up tents and sleeping bags.

Soon everything was on the trailer and Julian made them safe with ropes. They said goodbye to the watching grown-ups and climbed excitedly into the car. Mr Luffy started up his engine and put the lever into first gear with a terrible noise.

'Goodbye!' called all the grown-ups, and Julian's mother added a last word. 'DON'T get into any awful adventures this time!'

'Of course they won't!' called back Mr Luffy cheerfully. 'I'll see to that. There are no adventures to be found on a wild and deserted moor.

Goodbye!'

Off they went, waving madly, and shouting goodbye all the way down the road. 'Goodbye! Goodbyeeeeee! We're off at last!'

The car raced down the road, the trailer bumping madly after it. The holiday had begun!

2 Up on the moors

Mr Luffy wasn't a good driver. He went too fast, especially around the corners, and many times Julian looked behind at the trailer in alarm, afraid that everything would suddenly leap off it at some sharp bend.

He saw the bundle of sleeping bags jump high into the air, but fortunately they remained on the trailer.

'Sir! Could you go a bit slower, please?' he asked. 'The trailer will be empty by the time we arrive, if the luggage leaps about on it much more.'

'I forgot we had a trailer!' said Mr Luffy, slowing down at once. 'Remind me if I go too fast again, will you? Last time I took the trailer with me, I arrived with only half the goods on it. I don't want that to happen again.'

Julian certainly hoped it wouldn't. He kept a sharp eye on the speedometer, and when it went too high he reminded Mr Luffy to slow down.

Mr Luffy looked supremely happy. He didn't like term time, but he loved holidays. Term time interfered with the study of his beloved insect-world. Now he was off with four nice children he liked, for a holiday on a moorland he knew was alive with bees, beetles, butterflies and every other kind of insect he wanted. He looked forward to teaching the four children quite a lot. They would have been horrified if they guessed this.

He was an odd-looking man. He had very untidy, shaggy eyebrows over kind and gentle brown eyes that always reminded Dick of a monkey's. He had a large nose, which looked fiercer than it was because, unexpectedly, it had a forest of hairs growing out of the nostrils. He had an untidy moustache, and a round chin with a surprising dimple in the middle of it.

His ears always fascinated Anne. They were large and turned forward, and Mr Luffy could waggle the right one if he wanted to. To his great sorrow he'd never been able to waggle the left one. His hair was thick and untidy, and his clothes always looked loose, comfortable and too big for him.

The children liked him. They couldn't help it. He was so odd and gentle and untidy and forgetful – and yet sometimes unexpectedly fierce. Julian had often told them the story of Tom Killin the bully.

Mr Luffy had once found Tom bullying a small new boy in the cloakroom, dragging him around it by his belt. With a roar like an angry bull, Mr Luffy had pounced on the big bully, lifted him up and hooked his belt over a peg in the cloakroom.

'There you stay till you get someone to lift you down!' Mr Luffy had thundered. '*I* can get hold of a belt too, as you can see!'

And then he'd stalked out of the cloakroom with the small, terrified boy beside him, leaving the bully hung up high on the peg, unable to free himself. And there he had to stay, because not one of the boys who came pouring in from a game of football would lift him down.

'If the peg hadn't given way under his weight, he'd still be stuck up there,' Julian had said with a grin. 'Good old Mr Luffy! You'd never think he could be fierce like that, would you?'

Anne loved that story. Mr Luffy became a hero to her after that. She was pleased to sit next to him in the car, and chatter about all kinds of things. The other three were squashed at the back with Timmy on their feet. George stopped him from climbing up on her knee because it was so hot. So he contented himself with trying to stand up with his paws on the window-ledge and his nose over the side.

They stopped at about half past twelve for lunch. Mr Luffy had indeed brought sandwiches for everyone. And very good ones they were too, made the evening before by Mrs Luffy.

'Cucumber, dipped in vinegar! Ham and lettuce! Egg! Sardine! Oooh, Mr Luffy, your sandwiches are much nicer than ours,' said Anne, beginning on two together, one cucumber and the other ham and lettuce.

They were all very hungry. Timmy had a bit from everyone, usually the last bite, and watched each sandwich eagerly till his turn came. Mr Luffy didn't seem to understand that Timmy had to have the last bite of any sandwich, so Timmy simply took it out of his hand, much to his surprise.

'A clever dog,' he said, and patted him. 'Knows what he wants and takes it. Very clever.'

That pleased George, of course. She thought that Timmy was the cleverest dog in the world, and indeed it did seem like it at times. He understood every word she said to him, every pat, every stroke, every gesture. He'd be much, much better at keeping an eye on the four children and guarding them than forgetful Mr Luffy.

They drank ginger beer and then ate some ripe plums. Timmy wouldn't have any plums, but he licked up some spilt ginger beer. Then he snuffed up a few odd crumbs and went to drink at a little stream nearby.

The party set off again in the car. Anne fell asleep. Dick gave an enormous yawn and fell asleep too. George wasn't sleepy, nor was Timmy, but Julian was. He didn't dare to take his eye off the speedometer, though, because Mr Luffy seemed to be inclined to speed along too fast again, after his good lunch.

'We won't stop for tea till we get there,' said Mr Luffy suddenly, and Dick woke up with a jump at the sound of his booming voice. 'We should be there about half past five. Look, you can see the moorland in the distance now – all ablaze with heather!'

Everybody looked ahead, except Anne, who was still fast asleep. Rising up to the left for miles upon miles was the heather-covered moorland, a lovely sight to see. It looked wild and lonely and beautiful, blazing with heather, and shading off into a purple-blue in the distance.

'We take this road to the left, and then we're on the moors,' said Mr Luffy, swinging violently to the left, and making the luggage in the trailer jump high again. 'Here we go.'

The car climbed the high moorland road steadily. It passed one or two small houses, and in the distance the children could see little farms in clearings. Sheep dotted the moorland, and some of them stood staring at the car as it drove by.

'We've got about twenty miles to go, I think,' said Mr Luffy, jamming on his brakes suddenly to avoid two large sheep in the middle of the road. 'I wish these creatures wouldn't choose the centre of the road to gossip in. Hey, move on there! Let me pass!'

Timmy yelped and tried to get out of the car. The sheep hurriedly decided to move, and the car went on. Anne was thoroughly awake by now, having been almost jerked out of her seat by the sudden stop.

'What a shame to wake you!' said Mr Luffy, gazing down at her kindly, and almost running into a ditch by the side of the road. 'We're nearly there, Anne.'

They climbed steadily, and the wind grew a little cold. All around the children the moors stretched for mile upon mile, never-ending. Little streams sometimes splashed right down to the roadway, and ran beside it.

'We can drink the water in these streams,' said Mr Luffy. 'Crystal clear, and cold as ice! There's one quite near where we're going to camp.'

That was good news. Julian thought of the big buckets they'd brought. He didn't particularly want to carry those for miles. If there was a stream near their camping place it'd be easy to get the buckets filled with water.

The road forked into two. To the right was a good road, leading on and on. To the left it became not much more than a cart-track.

'That's the one we take,' said Mr Luffy, and the car jerked and jolted over it. He was forced to go slowly, and the children had time to see every little thing they passed.

'I'll leave the car here,' said Mr Luffy, bringing it to a standstill beside a great rock that stood up bare and grey out of the moor. 'It'll be sheltered from the worst winds and rain. I thought we'd camp over there.'

There was a little slope just there, backed by some enormous gorse bushes. Thick heather grew everywhere. Julian nodded. It was a good place for camping. Those thick gorse bushes would provide good shelter from the winds.

'Right, sir,' he said. 'Shall we have tea first, or unpack now?'

'Tea first,' said Mr Luffy. 'I've brought a very good little stove for boiling and cooking things. Better than a wood fire. That makes kettles and saucepans so black.'

'We've got a stove, too,' said Anne. She scrambled out of the car and looked all around. 'It's lovely here – all heather and wind and sun! Is that the farm over there – the one we'll go to for eggs and things?'

She pointed to a tiny farmhouse on the hill opposite. It stood in a small clearing. In a field behind it were three or four cows and a horse. A small orchard stood at the side, and a vegetable garden lay in front. It seemed odd to see such a trim little place in the midst of the moorland.

'That's Olly's Farm,' said Mr Luffy. 'It's changed hands, I believe, since I was here three years ago. I hope the new people are nice. Now – did we leave something to eat for our tea?'

They had, because Anne had wisely put away a good many sandwiches and bits of cake for tea-time. They sat in the heather, with bees humming all around them, and munched solidly for fifteen minutes. Timmy waited patiently for his bits, watching the bees that hummed around him. There were thousands of them.

'And now I suppose we'd better put up our tents,' said Julian. 'Come on, let's unpack the trailer. Mr Luffy, we don't intend to camp on top of you, sir, because you won't want four noisy children too near. Where would you like your tent put?'

Mr Luffy was about to say that he'd like to have the four children and Timmy quite close, when it suddenly occurred to him that perhaps they might not want him too near. They might want to make a noise, or play silly games, and if he were near it would stop them enjoying themselves in their own way.

So he made up his mind not to be too close.

'I'll pitch my tent down there, where that old gorse bush is,' he said. 'And if you'd like to put yours up here, where there's a half-circle of gorse bushes keeping off the wind, you'd be well sheltered. And we won't interfere with one another at all.'

'Right, sir,' said Julian, and he and the others began to tackle the tents.

It was fun. Timmy got under everyone's feet as usual, and ran off with an important rope, but nobody minded.

By the time that dusk came creeping up the heather-covered moorland, all three tents were up, the groundsheets were put down, and the sleeping bags unrolled on them, two in each of the children's tents, and one in Mr Luffy's.

'I'm going to turn in,' said Mr Luffy. 'My eyes are almost shut. Goodnight all of you. Sleep well!'

He disappeared into the dusk. Anne yawned widely, and that set the others off too. 'Come on – let's turn in, too,' said Julian. 'We'll have a bar of chocolate each, and a few biscuits. We can eat those in our sleeping bags. Goodnight, girls. Won't it be wonderful to wake up tomorrow morning?'

He and Dick disappeared into their tent. The girls crawled into theirs with Timmy. They undressed, and got into their warm, soft sleeping bags.

'This is great!' said George, pushing Timmy to one side. 'I've never felt so cosy in my life. *Don't* do that, Timmy. Don't you know the difference between my feet and my middle? That's better.'

'Goodnight,' said Anne, sleepily. 'Look, George, you can see the stars shining through the opening of the tent. Don't they look enormous?'

But George didn't care whether they were enormous or not. She was fast asleep, tired out with the day's run. Timmy pricked up one ear when he heard Anne's voice, and gave a little grunt. That was his way of saying goodnight. Then he put his head down and slept.

'Our first night of camping,' thought Anne, happily. 'I won't go to sleep. I'll lie awake and look at the stars and smell that heathery smell.'

But she didn't. In half a second she was fast asleep, too!

3 Anne's volcano

Julian awoke first in the morning. He heard a strange and lonely sound floating overhead. 'Coor-lie! Coor-lie!'

He sat up and wondered where he was and who was calling. Of course! He was in his tent with Dick – they were camping on the moors. And that wild cry overhead came from a curlew, the bird of the moorlands.

He yawned and lay down again. It was early in the morning. The sun put its warm fingers in at his tent opening, and he felt the warmth on his sleeping bag. He felt lazy and snug and contented. He also felt hungry, which was a nuisance. He glanced at his watch.

Half past six. He really was too warm and comfortable to get up yet. He put out his hand to see if there was any chocolate left from the night before, and found a little piece. He put it into his mouth and lay there contentedly, listening to more curlews, and watching the sun climb a little higher.

He fell asleep again, and was awakened by Timmy busily licking his face. He sat up with a start. The girls were peering in at his tent, grinning. They were fully dressed already.

'Wake up, lazy!' said Anne. 'We sent Timmy in to get you up. It's half past seven. We've been up for ages.'

'It's a gorgeous morning,' said George. 'Going to be a really hot day. Do get up. We're going to find the stream and wash in it. It seems silly to lug heavy buckets of water to and fro for washing, if the stream's nearby.'

Dick awoke too. He and Julian decided to go and take a swim in the stream. They wandered out into the sunny morning, feeling very happy and very hungry. The girls were just coming back from the stream.

'It's over there,' said Anne, pointing. 'Timmy, go with them and show them. It's a lovely little stream, very cold, and it's got ferns along its banks. We've left the bucket there. Bring it back full, will you?'

'What do you want us to do that for, if you've

already washed?' asked Dick.

'We want water for washing up the dishes,' said Anne. 'I suddenly remembered we'd need water for that. Hey, do you think we ought to wake up Mr Luffy? There's no sign of him yet.'

'No, let him sleep,' said Julian. 'He's probably tired out with driving the car so slowly! We can easily save him some breakfast. What are we going to have?'

'We've unpacked some bacon rashers and tomatoes,' said Anne, who loved cooking. 'How do you light the stove, Julian?'

'George knows,' said Julian. 'Oh, did we pack a frying pan?'

'Yes. I packed it myself,' said Anne. 'Go and swim if you're going to. Breakfast will be ready before you are!'

Timmy gravely trotted off with the boys and showed them the stream. Julian and Dick at once lay down in the clear water, and kicked wildly. Timmy leapt in too, and there were yells and shrieks.

'Well – I expect we've woken up Mr Luffy now!' said Dick, rubbing himself down with a rough towel. 'How lovely and cold that was. The trouble is it's made me feel twice as hungry!'

'Doesn't that frying bacon smell good?' said Julian, sniffing the air.

They walked back to the girls. There was still no sign of Mr Luffy. He must sleep very soundly!

They sat down in the heather and began their breakfast. Anne had fried big rounds of bread in with the bacon and tomatoes, and the boys told her she was the best cook in the world. She was very pleased.

'I'll look after the food side for you,' she said. 'But everyone must help with the preparing of the meals and washing up. All right?'

The boys agreed, but George looked sulky. She hated doing all the things that Anne loved to do, such as making beds and washing up.

'Look at George! Why bother about the washing up when there's Timmy only too pleased to use his tongue to wash every plate?' said Dick.

Everyone laughed, even George.

'All right,' she said, 'I'll help too, of course. Only let's use as few plates as possible, then there won't be much washing up. Is there any more fried bread, Anne?'

'No. But there are some biscuits in that tin,'

said Anne. 'Who's going to go to the farm each day for milk and things? I expect they can let us have bread, too, and fruit.'

'Oh, one or other of us will go,' said Dick. 'Anne, hadn't you better fry something for Mr Luffy now? I'll go and wake him. Half the day will be gone if he doesn't get up now.'

'I'll go and make a noise like an earwig outside his tent,' said Julian, getting up. 'He might not wake with all our yells and shouts, but he'd certainly wake at the call of a friendly earwig!'

He went down to the tent. He cleared his throat and called politely: 'Are you awake yet, sir?'

There was no answer. Julian called again. Then, puzzled, he went to the tent opening. The flap was closed. He pulled it aside and looked in.

The tent was empty! There was nobody there at all.

'What's up, Ju?' called Dick.

'He's not here,' said Julian. 'Where can he be?'

There was silence. For a panic-stricken moment Anne thought one of their strange adventures was beginning. Then Dick called out again: 'Is his bug-tin gone? You know, the tin box with straps that he takes with him when he goes insect-hunting? And what about his clothes?'

Julian inspected the inside of the tent again. 'Yes!' he called, much to everyone's relief. 'His clothes are gone, and so has his bug-tin. He must have slipped out early before we were awake. I bet he's forgotten all about us and breakfast and everything!'

'That'd be just like him,' said Dick. 'Well, we're not his keepers. He can do as he likes! If he doesn't want breakfast, he needn't have any. He'll come back when he's finished his hunting, I suppose.'

'Anne! Can you get on with the washing up if Dick and I go to the farmhouse and see what food they've got?' asked Julian. 'The time's getting on, and if we're going for a walk or anything today, we don't want to start too late.'

'Right,' said Anne. 'You go too, George. I can manage everything, now that the boys have brought me a bucketful of water. Take Timmy. He wants a walk.'

George was only too pleased to get out of the washing up. She and the boys, with Timmy trotting in front, set off to the farmhouse.

Anne got on with her jobs, humming softly to herself in the sunshine. She soon finished them, and then looked to see if the others were coming back. There was no sign of them, or of Mr Luffy either.

'I'll go for a walk on my own,' thought Anne. 'I'll follow that little stream uphill and see where it begins. That'd be fun. I can't possibly lose my way if I keep by the water.'

She set off in the sunshine and came to the little stream that gurgled down the hill. She scrambled through the heather beside it, following its course uphill. She liked all the little green ferns and the cushions of velvety moss that edged it. She tasted the water – it was cold and sweet and clean.

Feeling very happy all by herself, Anne walked on and on. She came at last to a big mound of a hilltop. The little stream began there, halfway up the mound. It came gurgling out of the heathery hillside, edged with moss, and made its chattering way far down the hill.

'So that's where you begin, is it?' said Anne. She flung herself down on the heather, hot with her climb. It was nice there, with the sun on her face, and the sound of the trickling water nearby.

She lay listening to the humming bees and the water. And then she heard another sound. She took no notice of it at all at first.

Then she sat up, frightened. 'The noise is underground! Deep, deep underground! It rumbles and roars. Oh, what's going to happen? Is there going to be an earthquake?'

The rumbling seemed to come nearer and nearer. Anne didn't even dare to get up and run. She sat there and trembled.

Then there came an unearthly shriek, and not far off an astonishing thing happened. A great cloud of white smoke came right out of the ground and hung in the air before the wind blew it away. Anne was terrified. It was so sudden, so very unexpected on this quiet hillside. The rumbling noise went on for a while and then gradually faded away.

Anne leapt to her feet in a panic. She fled down the hill, screaming loudly: 'It's a volcano! Help! Help! I've been sitting on a volcano. It's going to burst, it's sending out smoke. Help, help, it's a VOLCANO!'

She ran down the hillside, caught her foot on a tuft of heather and went rolling over and over, sobbing. She came to rest at last, and then heard an anxious voice calling:

'Who's that? What's the matter?'

It was Mr Luffy's voice. Anne screamed to him in relief. 'Mr Luffy! Come and save me! There's a volcano here!'

There was such terror in her voice that Mr Luffy came racing to her at once. He sat down beside the trembling girl and put his arm around her.

'Whatever's the matter?' he said. 'What's frightened you?'

Anne told him again. 'Up there – do you see? That's a volcano, Mr Luffy. It trembled and rumbled and then it shot up clouds of smoke. Oh quick, before it sends out red hot lava!'

'Now, now!' said Mr Luffy, and to Anne's surprise and relief he actually laughed. 'Do you mean to tell me you don't know what that was?'

'No, I don't,' said Anne.

'Well,' said Mr Luffy, 'under this big moor run two or three long tunnels to take special steam-trains from one valley to another. Didn't you know? They make the rumbling noise you heard, and the sudden smoke you saw was the smoke sent up by a train below. There are big vent-holes here and there in the moor for the smoke to escape from.'

'Oh, silly me!' said Anne, going red. 'I didn't even *know* there were trains under here. What an amazing thing! I really did think I was sitting on a volcano, Mr Luffy. You won't tell the others, will you? They'd laugh at me so much.'

'I won't say a word,' said Mr Luffy. 'And now I think we'll go back. Have you had breakfast? I'm very hungry. I went out early after a rare butterfly I saw flying by my tent.'

'We had breakfast *ages* ago,' said Anne. 'But if you'd like to come back with me now I'll cook you some bacon, Mr Luffy. And some tomatoes and fried bread.'

'Aha! It sounds good,' said Mr Luffy. 'Now – not a word about volcanoes. That's our secret.'

And off they went to the tents, where the others were wondering what in the world had become of Anne. Little did they know she'd been 'sitting on a volcano'!

4 Spook-trains

The boys and George were full of talk about the farm.

'It's a nice little place,' said Julian, sitting down while Anne began to cook breakfast for Mr Luffy. 'Pretty farmhouse, nice little dairy, well-kept sheds. And even a grand piano in the sitting room.'

'Really? You wouldn't think they'd make enough money to buy a thing like that, would you?' said Anne, turning over the bacon in the pan.

'The farmer's got a very nice car,' went on Julian. 'Brand new. Must have cost him a fortune. His son showed it to us. And he showed us some really good new farm machinery too.'

'Very interesting,' said Mr Luffy. 'I wonder how they make their money, farming that bit of land? The last people were hard-working folk, but they certainly couldn't have afforded a new car or a grand piano.'

'And you should have seen the lorries they've got!' said Dick. 'Beauties! The son said his dad's going to use them for carting things from the farm to the market.'

'What things?' said Mr Luffy, looking across at the little farmhouse. 'I wouldn't have thought they needed an army of lorries for that! An old farm van would carry all *their* produce.'

'Well, that's what he told us,' said Dick. 'Everything certainly looked very expensive. He must be a very good farmer.'

'We got eggs and butter and fruit, and even some bacon,' said George. 'The boy's mum didn't seem worried about how much we had, and she hardly charged us anything. We didn't see the farmer.'

Mr Luffy was now eating his breakfast. He was certainly very hungry. He brushed away the flies that hung around his head, and when one settled on his right ear he waggled it violently. The fly flew off in surprise.

'Oh, do that again!' begged Anne. 'How do you do it? Do you think if I practised hard for weeks I could make my ear move?'

'No, I don't think so,' said Mr Luffy, finishing his breakfast. 'Well, I've got some writing to do now. What are you going to do? Go for a walk?'

'We might as well take a picnic lunch and go off somewhere,' said Julian. 'How about that?'

'Yes,' said Dick. 'Let's pack lunch and tea. What about hard-boiled eggs?'

It wasn't long before they had a picnic meal packed in greaseproof paper.

'You won't get lost, will you?' said Mr Luffy.

'No, sir,' said Julian, with a laugh. 'I've got a compass, anyway, and a good sense of direction, too. I usually know the way to go. We'll see you this evening, when we get back.'

'*You* won't get lost, Mr Luffy, will you?' asked Anne, looking worried.

'Don't be cheeky, Anne,' said Dick, horrified at Anne's question. But she really meant it. Mr Luffy was so absent-minded that she could imagine him wandering off and not being able to find his way back.

He smiled at her.

'No,' he said. 'I know my way around here all right – I know every stream and path and er – volcano!'

Anne giggled. The others stared at Mr Luffy, wondering what he meant, but neither he nor Anne told them. They said goodbye and set off.

'It's lovely walking today,' said Anne. 'Shall we follow a path if we find one or not?'

'Might as well,' said Julian. 'It'll be a bit tiring scrambling through heather all the day.'

So when they did unexpectedly come across a path they followed it.

'It's just a shepherd's path, I expect,' said Dick. 'I bet it's a lonely job, looking after sheep up on these heathery hills.'

They went on for some way, enjoying the stretches of bright heather, the lizards that darted quickly away from their feet and the hosts of butterflies of all kinds that hovered and fluttered. Anne loved the little blue ones best and made up her mind to ask Mr Luffy what all their names were.

They had their lunch on a hilltop overlooking a vast stretch of heather, with grey-white blobs in it here and there – the sheep that wandered everywhere.

And, in the very middle of the meal, Anne heard the same rumbling she'd heard before, and then, not far off, out spouted some white smoke from the ground. George went very pale. Timmy leapt to his feet, growling and barking, his tail down.

The boys roared with laughter. 'It's all right, Anne and George. It's only the trains underground here. We knew they ran under the moors and we thought we'd see what you did when you first heard them rumbling, and saw the smoke.'

'I'm not frightened,' said Anne, and the boys looked at her, astonished. It was George who was the scared one! Usually it was the other way round.

George got back her colour and laughed. She called Timmy. 'It's all right, Tim. Come here. You know what trains are, don't you?'

The children discussed the trains. It seemed strange to think of trains in those hollowed-out tunnels down below the moors – the people in them, reading their newspapers and talking – down in tunnels where the sun never shone at all.

'Come on,' said Julian, at last. 'Let's go on. We'll walk to the top of the next slope, and then I think we ought to turn back.'

They found a little path that Julian said must

be a rabbit-path, because it was so narrow, and set off, chattering and laughing. They climbed through the heather to the top of the next slope. And at the top they got a big surprise.

Down in the valley below was a silent and deserted stretch of railway lines! They appeared out of the black hole of a tunnel-mouth, ran for about half a mile, and then ended in what seemed to be a kind of railway yard.

'Look at that,' said Julian. 'Old derelict lines – not used any more, I expect. I bet that tunnel's out of date, too.'

'Let's go down and have a look,' said Dick. 'Come on! We've got plenty of time, and we can easily go back a shorter way.'

They set off down the hill to the lines. They arrived some way from the tunnel-mouth, and followed the lines to the deserted railway yard. There seemed to be nobody around at all.

'Look,' said Dick, 'there are some old wagons on that set of lines over there. They look as if they haven't been used for a hundred years. Let's give them a shove and set them going!'

'Oh, no!' said Anne, afraid. But the two boys and George, who had always longed to play about with real railway trucks, ran over to where three or four stood on the lines. Dick and Julian shoved hard at one. It moved. It ran a little way and crashed into the buffers of another. It made a terrific noise in the silent yard.

A door flew open in a tiny hut at the side of the yard, and a terrifying figure came out. It was a one-legged man, with a wooden peg for his other leg, two great arms that could easily have belonged to a gorilla, and a face as red as a tomato, except where grey stubble grew.

He opened his mouth and the children expected a loud and angry yell. Instead out came a husky, hoarse whisper:

'What you doing? Ain't it bad enough to hear spook-trains running at night, without hearing them in the daytime, too?'

The four children stared at him. He came nearer to them, and his wooden leg tip-tapped oddly. He swung his great arms loosely. He peered at the children as if he could hardly see them.

'I've broken me glasses,' he said, and two tears ran down his cheeks. 'Poor old Wooden-Leg Sam, he's broken his glasses. Nobody cares about Wooden-Leg Sam now, nobody at all.'

There didn't seem anything to say to all this. Anne felt sorry for the man, but she kept well behind Julian.

Sam peered at them again. 'Haven't you got tongues in your heads? Am I seeing things again, or are you there?'

'We're here and we're real,' said Julian. 'We happened to see this old railway yard and we came down to have a look at it. Who are you?'

'I told you – I'm Wooden-Leg Sam,' said the man impatiently. 'I'm the watchman. Although what there is to watch here beats me. Do they think I'm going to watch for these spook-trains? Well, I'm not. Not me, Wooden-Leg Sam. I've seen many strange things in my life, yes, and been scared by them too, and I'm not watching for any more spook-trains.'

The children listened curiously. 'What spook-trains?' asked Julian.

Wooden-Leg Sam came closer. He looked all around as if he thought there might be someone listening, and then spoke in a hoarser whisper than usual.

'Spook-trains, I tell you. Trains that come out of that tunnel at night all by themselves, and go back all by themselves. Nobody in them. One night they'll come for old Wooden-Leg Sam – but, see, I'm clever, I am. I lock myself into my hut and get under the bed. And I turn my light out so those spook-trains don't know I'm there.'

Anne shivered. She pulled at Julian's hand. 'Julian! Let's go. I don't like it. It sounds horrible. What does he mean?'

The man seemed suddenly to change his mood. He picked up a large clod of earth and threw it at Dick, hitting him on the head. 'You clear out! I'm watchman here. And what did they tell me? They told me to chase away anyone that came. Clear out, I tell you!'

In terror Anne fled away. Timmy growled and would have leapt at the strange watchman, but George had her hand on his collar. Dick rubbed his head where the clod of earth had hit him.

'We're going,' he said soothingly to Sam. 'We didn't mean to trespass. You look after your spook-trains. We won't bother you!'

The boys and George turned away, and caught up with Anne. 'What did he mean?' she asked, scared. 'What are spook-trains? Trains that aren't real? Does he really see them at night?'

'He just imagines them,' said Julian. 'I expect being there all alone in that deserted old railway yard has made him think strange things. Don't worry, Anne. There are no such things as spook-trains.'

'But he spoke as if there were,' said Anne. 'He really did. I'd hate to see a spook-train. Wouldn't you, Ju?'

'No. I'd *love* to see one,' said Julian, and he turned to Dick. 'Wouldn't you, Dick? Shall we come one night and watch? Just to see?'

5 Back at camp again

The children and Timmy left the deserted railway yard behind them and climbed up the heathery slope to find their way back to their camping place. The boys couldn't stop talking about Wooden-Leg Sam and the strange things he said.

'It's all a bit strange,' said Julian. 'I wonder why that yard isn't used any more – and where that tunnel leads to – and if trains ever do run there.'

'I expect there's an ordinary explanation,' said Dick. 'It's just that Wooden-Leg Sam made it all seem so odd. If there had been a proper watchman we wouldn't have thought there was anything strange about it at all.'

'Perhaps the boy at the farm would know,' said Julian. 'We'll ask him tomorrow. I'm afraid there aren't any spook-trains really – but I'd love to go and watch for one, if there were any.'

'I wish you wouldn't talk like that,' said Anne, unhappily. 'You know, it makes me feel as if you want another adventure. And I don't.'

'There won't be any adventure, so don't worry,' said Dick, comfortingly. 'And, anyway, if there was an adventure you could always go and hold Mr Luffy's hand. He wouldn't see an adventure if it was right under his nose. You'd be safe with him.'

'Look – who's that up there?' said George, seeing Timmy prick up his ears, and then hearing him give a little growl.

'Shepherd or something, I expect,' said Julian. He shouted out cheerfully. 'Hello! Nice day it's been!'

The man on the path just above them nodded his head. He was either a shepherd or farm labourer of some sort. He waited for them to come up.

'Have you seen any of my sheep down along there?' he asked them. 'They've got red crosses on them.'

'No. There aren't any down there,' said Julian. 'But there are some farther along the hill. We've been down to the railway yard and we'd have seen any sheep on the slope below.'

'Don't you go down there,' said the shepherd,

his faded blue eyes looking into Julian's. 'That's a bad place, that is.'

'Well, we've been hearing about spook-trains!' said Julian, with a laugh. 'Is that what you mean?'

'Yes. There are trains that nobody knows of running out of that tunnel,' said the shepherd. 'Many's the time I've heard them when I've been up here at night with my sheep. That tunnel hasn't been used for thirty years – but the trains, they still come out of it, just as they used to.'

'How do you know? Have you seen them?' asked Julian, a cold shiver creeping down his spine.

'No. I've only heard them,' said the old man. 'Choo, choo, they go, and they jangle and clank. But they don't whistle any more. Old Wooden-Leg Sam reckons they're spook-trains, with nobody to drive them and nobody to tend them. Don't you go down to that place. It's bad and scary.'

Julian caught sight of Anne's scared face. He laughed loudly. 'What a tale! I don't believe in spook-trains. Dick, have you got the tea in your bag? Let's find a nice place and have some sandwiches and cake. Will you join us, sir?'

'No, but thank you,' said the man, moving off.

'I'll be after my sheep. Always wandering they are, and they keep me wandering, too. Goodbye, and don't go down to that bad place.'

Julian found a good spot out of sight of 'that bad place', and they all sat down.

'All a lot of nonsense,' said Julian, who wanted Anne to feel happier again. 'We can easily ask the farmer's boy about it tomorrow. I expect it's all a silly story made up by that watchman, and passed on to the shepherd.'

'I expect so,' said Dick. 'Did you notice that the shepherd had never actually *seen* the trains, Julian? Only heard them. Well, sound travels far at night, and I expect what he heard was the rumblings of the trains that go underground here. There's one going somewhere now! I can feel the ground trembling!'

They all could. It was a strange feeling. The rumbling stopped at last and they sat and ate their tea, watching Timmy scraping at a rabbit-hole and trying his hardest to get down it. He covered them with sandy soil as he burrowed, and nothing would stop him. He seemed to have gone completely deaf.

'If we don't get Timmy out of that hole now

he'll be gone down so far that we'll have to drag him out by his tail,' said Julian, getting up. 'Timmy! TIMMY! The rabbit's miles away. Come out.'

It took both George and Julian to get him out. He was very indignant. He looked at them as if to say: '*Well*, what spoilsports! Almost got him and you drag me out!'

He shook himself, and bits of grit and sand flew out of his hair. He took a step towards the hole again, but George caught hold of his tail. 'No, Timmy. Home now!'

'He's looking for a spook-train,' said Dick, and that made everyone laugh, even Anne.

They set off back to the camping place, pleasantly tired, with Timmy following sulkily at their heels. When they at last got back they saw Mr Luffy sitting waiting for them. The blue smoke from his pipe curled up into the air.

'Hello, hello!' he said, and his brown eyes looked up at them from under his shaggy eyebrows. 'I was beginning to wonder if you'd got lost. Still, I suppose that dog of yours would always bring you back.'

Timmy wagged his tail politely. 'Woof,' he

agreed, and went to drink out of the bucket of water. Anne stopped him just in time.

'No, Timmy! Don't drink out of our washing-up water. There's yours, in the dish over there.'

Timmy went to his dish and lapped. He thought Anne was very fussy. Anne asked Mr Luffy if he'd like any supper.

'We're not having a proper supper,' she said. 'We had tea so late. But I'll cook you something if you like, Mr Luffy.'

'Very kind of you. But I've had an enormous tea,' said Mr Luffy. 'I've brought up a fruitcake for you, from my larder. Shall we share it for supper? And I've got a bottle of lime cordial, too, which will taste lovely with some of the stream water.'

The boys went off to get some fresh stream water for drinking. Anne got out some plates and cut slices of the cake.

'Well,' said Mr Luffy. 'Had a nice walk?'

'Yes,' said Anne, 'except that we met a strange one-legged man who told us he saw spook-trains.'

Mr Luffy laughed. 'He must be a cousin of a little girl I know who thought she was sitting on a volcano.'

Anne giggled. 'Don't tease me. No, honestly, Mr Luffy, this old man was a watchman at a sort of old railway yard – not used now – and he said when the spook-trains came, he turned out his light and got under his bed so that they wouldn't get him.'

'Poor old thing,' said Mr Luffy. 'I hope he didn't frighten you.'

'He did a bit,' said Anne. 'And he threw some earth at Dick and hit him on the head. Tomorrow we're going to the farm to ask the boy there if he's heard of the spook-trains, too. We met a shepherd who said he'd heard them but not seen them.'

'It all sounds very interesting,' said Mr Luffy. 'But these exciting stories usually have a very boring explanation, you know. Now would you like to see what I found today? A very rare and interesting little beetle.'

He opened a small square tin and showed a shiny beetle to Anne. It had green feelers and a red fiery spot near its tail-end. It was a lovely little thing.

'Now that's much more exciting to me than half a dozen spook-trains,' he told Anne. 'Spook-trains won't keep me awake at night – but thinking of this little beetle here certainly will.'

'I don't very much like beetles,' said Anne. 'But this one is pretty. Do you really like hunting about all day for insects, and watching them, Mr Luffy?'

'Yes, very much,' said Mr Luffy. 'Ah, here come the boys with the water. Now we'll hand the cake around, shall we? Where's George? Oh, there she is, changing her shoes.'

George had a blister, and she'd been putting a plaster on her heel. She came up when the boys arrived and the cake was handed round. They sat in a circle, munching, while the sun gradually went down in a blaze of red.

'Nice day tomorrow again,' said Julian. 'What shall we do?'

'We'll have to go to the farm first,' said Dick. 'The farmer's wife said she'd let us have some more bread if we turned up in the morning. And we could do with more eggs if we can get them. We took eight hard-boiled ones with us today and we've only one or two left. And who's eaten all the tomatoes?'

'All of you,' said Anne at once. 'You're pigs over the tomatoes.'

'I'm afraid I'm one of the pigs,' apologised Mr Luffy. 'I think you fried me six for my breakfast, Anne.'

'That's all right,' said Anne. 'You didn't have as many as the others, even so! We can easily get some more.'

It was pleasant sitting there, eating and talking, and drinking lime cordial and stream water. They were all tired, and it was nice to think of the cosy sleeping bags. Timmy lifted his head and gave a vast yawn, showing an enormous amount of teeth.

'Timmy! I could see right down to your tail then!' said George. 'Do shut your mouth up. You've made us all yawn.'

So he had. Even Mr Luffy was yawning. He got up. 'Well, I'm going to turn in,' he said. 'Goodnight. We'll make plans tomorrow morning. I'll bring up some breakfast for you, if you like. I've got some tins of sardines.'

'Oh, thanks,' said Anne. 'And there's some of this cake left. I hope you won't think that's too funny a breakfast, Mr Luffy – sardines and fruit cake?'

'Not at all. It sounds like a very sensible meal,'

came Mr Luffy's voice from down the hillside. 'Goodnight!'

The children sat there a few minutes longer. The sun went right out of sight. The wind grew a little chilly. Timmy yawned enormously again.

'Come on,' said Julian. 'Time we turned in. I'm glad Timmy didn't come into our tent and walk all over me last night. Goodnight, girls. It's going to be a nice night – but as I'll be asleep in about two seconds, I won't see much of it!'

The girls went into their tent. They were soon in their sleeping bags. Just before they went to sleep Anne felt the slight shivering of the earth that meant a train was running underground somewhere. She could hear no rumbling sound. She fell asleep thinking of it.

The boys were not asleep. They, too, had felt the trembling of the earth beneath them, and it had reminded them of the old railway yard.

'Funny about those spook-trains, Dick,' said Julian, sleepily. 'Wonder if there's anything in it?'

'No. How could there be?' said Dick. 'All the same we'll go to the farm tomorrow and have a chat with that boy. He lives on the moors and he ought to know the truth.'

'The truth is that Wooden-Leg Sam is a bit mad, and imagines things, and the shepherd is ready to believe in anything strange,' said Julian.

'I expect you're right,' said Dick. 'Oh, what's that?'

A dark shape stood looking in at the tent-flap. It gave a little whine.

'Oh, it's you, Timmy. Would you mind *not* coming and pretending you're a spook-train or something?' said Dick. 'And if you dare to put so much as half a paw on my middle, I'll scare you down the hill with a roar like a man-eating tiger. Go away.'

Timmy put a paw on Julian. Julian yelled out to George. 'George! Call this dog of yours, will you? He's just about to turn himself around twenty times on my middle, and curl himself up for the night.'

There was no answer from George. Timmy, feeling that he wasn't wanted, disappeared. He went back to George and curled himself up on her feet. He put his nose down on his paws and slept.

'Spooky Timmy,' murmured Julian, rearranging himself. 'Timmy spooky – no, I mean – oh dear, what do I mean?'

'Shut up,' said Dick. 'What with you and Timmy messing about, I can't get – to – sleep!' But he could and he did – almost before he'd finished speaking. Silence fell on the little camp, and nobody noticed when the next train rumbled underground – not even Timmy!

6 Day at the farm

The next day the children were up very early, as early as Mr Luffy, and they all had breakfast together. Mr Luffy had a map of the moorlands, and he studied it carefully after breakfast.

'I think I'll go off for the whole day,' he said to Julian, who was sitting beside him. 'See that little valley marked here – Crowleg Vale – well, I've heard that some of the rarest beetles in Britain can be found there. I think I'll take my gear and go along. What are you four going to do?'

'Five,' said George at once. 'You've forgotten Timmy.'

'So I have. I beg his pardon,' said Mr Luffy, solemnly. 'Well – what are you going to do?'

'We'll go over to the farm and get more food,' said Julian. 'And ask that boy if he's heard about the spook-trains. And perhaps look around the farm and get to know the animals there. I like farms.'

'Right,' said Mr Luffy, beginning to light his pipe. 'Don't worry about me if I'm not back till evening. When I'm bug-hunting I lose track of time.'

'You're sure you won't get lost?' said Anne, anxiously. She didn't really feel that Mr Luffy could take proper care of himself.

'Oh yes. My right ear always warns me if I'm losing my way,' said Mr Luffy. 'It waggles hard.'

He waggled it at Anne and she laughed.

'I wish you'd tell me how you do that,' she said. 'I'm sure you know. The girls at school would be so impressed if I learnt that trick. They'd think it was brilliant.'

Mr Luffy grinned and got up.

'Well, see you later,' he said. 'I'm off before Anne makes me give her a lesson in ear-waggles.'

He went off down the slope to his own tent. Dick and Anne washed up, while George and Julian tightened some tent ropes that had come loose, and generally tidied up.

'I suppose it's all right leaving everything unguarded like this?' said Anne, anxiously.

'Well, we did yesterday,' said Dick. 'And who's likely to come and take anything up here in this wild and lonely spot? You don't think a spook-train will come along and bundle everything into one of its carriages, do you, Anne?'

Anne giggled. 'Don't be silly. I just wondered if we ought to leave Timmy on guard, that's all.'

'Leave Timmy!' said George, amazed. 'You don't really think I'd leave Timmy behind every time we go off anywhere, Anne? Don't be silly.'

'No, I didn't really think you would,' said Anne. 'Well, I suppose nobody will come along here. Throw over that tea towel, Dick, if you've finished with it.'

Soon the tea towels were hanging over the gorse bushes to dry in the sun. Everything was put away neatly in the tents. Mr Luffy had called a loud goodbye and gone. Now the five were ready to go off to the farm.

Anne took a basket, and gave one to Julian too.

'To bring back the food,' she said. 'Are you ready to go now?'

They set off over the heather, their knees brushing through the honeyed flowers, and sending lots of busy bees into the air. It was a lovely day again, and the children felt free and happy.

They came to the little farm. A few men were in the fields, but Julian didn't think they looked as if they were working very hard. He looked around for the farmer's son.

The boy came out of a shed and whistled to them. 'Hello! You come for some more eggs? I've collected some for you.'

He stared at Anne. 'You didn't come yesterday. What's your name?'

'Anne,' said Anne. 'What's yours?'

'Jock,' said the boy, with a grin. He seemed nice, Anne thought, with straw-coloured hair, blue eyes, and a red face which looked very good-tempered.

'Where's your mum?' said Julian. 'Can we get some bread and other things from her today? We ate a lot of our food yesterday, and we want to stock up our larder again!'

'She's busy in the dairy,' said Jock. 'Are you in a hurry? Come and see my puppies.'

They all walked off with him to a shed. In there, right at the end, was a big box lined with straw. A collie dog lay there with five lovely little puppies. She growled at Timmy fiercely, and he backed hurriedly out of the shed. He'd met fierce mother-dogs before, and he didn't like them!

The four children exclaimed over the fat little puppies, and Anne took one out very gently. It cuddled into her arms and made funny little whining noises.

'I wish it was mine,' said Anne. 'I'd call it Cuddle.'

'What a horrible name for a dog,' said George scornfully. 'Just the kind of silly name you *would* think of, Anne. Let me hold it. Are they all yours, Jock?'

'Yes,' said Jock, proudly. 'The mother's mine, you see. Her name's Biddy.'

Biddy pricked up her ears at her name and looked up at Jock out of bright, alert eyes. He fondled her silky head.

'I've had her for four years,' he said. 'When we were at Owl Farm, Farmer Burrows gave her to me when she was eight weeks old.'

'Oh – were you at another farm before this one, then?' asked Anne. 'Have you always lived on a farm? Aren't you lucky!'

'I've only lived on two,' said Jock. 'Owl Farm and this one. Mum and I had to leave Owl Farm when Dad died, and we went to live in a town for a year. I hated that. I was glad when we came here.'

'But I thought your dad was here!' said Dick, puzzled.

'That's my stepfather,' said Jock. 'He's not a farmer, though!' He looked around and lowered his voice. 'He doesn't know much about farming. It's my mum that tells the men what to do. Still, he gives her plenty of money to do everything well, and we've got good machinery and wagons and things. Like to see the dairy? It's really modern and Mum loves working in it.'

Jock took the four children to the shining, spotless dairy. His mother was at work there with a helper. She nodded and smiled at the children. 'Good morning! Hungry again? I'll pack you up plenty of food when I've finished in the dairy. Would you like to stay and have lunch with Jock? He's lonely here in the holidays, with no other children to keep him company.'

'Oh, *yes* – let's!' cried Anne, in delight. 'I'd like that. Can we, Ju?'

'Yes. Thank you very much, Mrs – er – Mrs . . .' said Julian.

'I'm Mrs Andrews,' said Jock's mother. 'But

Jock is Jock Robins – he's the son of my first husband, a farmer. Well, stay to lunch all of you, and I'll see if I can give you a meal that'll keep you going for the rest of the day!'

This sounded good. The four children felt thrilled, and Timmy wagged his tail hard. He liked Mrs Andrews.

'Come on,' said Jock, joyfully. 'I'll take you all round the farm, into every corner. It's not very big, but we're going to make it the best little farm on the moorlands. My stepfather doesn't seem to take much interest in the work of the farm, but he's very generous when it comes to handing out money to Mum to buy everything she wants.'

It certainly seemed to the children that the machinery on the farm was absolutely up to date. They examined the combine, they went into the little cowshed and admired the clean stone floor with white brick walls, they climbed into the red-painted wagons, and they wished they could try the two tractors that stood side by side in a barn.

'You've got plenty of men here to work the farm,' said Julian. 'I wouldn't have thought there was enough for so many to do on this small place.'

'They're not good workers,' said Jock, frowning. 'Mum's always getting angry with them. They just don't know what to do. Dad gives her plenty of men to work the farm, but he always chooses the wrong ones! They don't seem to like farm work, and they're always running off to the nearest town whenever they can. There's only one good one and he's old. See him over there? His name's Will.'

The children looked at Will. He was working in the little vegetable garden, an old man with a shrivelled face, a tiny nose and a pair of very blue eyes. They liked the look of him.

'Yes. He *looks* like a farm worker,' said Julian. 'The others don't.'

'He won't work with them,' said Jock. 'He just complains about them, and calls them ninnies and idjits.'

'What's an idjit?' asked Anne.

'An idiot, silly,' said Dick. He walked up to Will.

'Good morning,' he said. 'You look very busy. There's always a lot to do on a farm, isn't there?'

The old man looked at Dick out of his very blue eyes, and went on with his work. 'Plenty to do and plenty of folk to do it, and not much done,' he said, in a croaking kind of voice. 'Never thought I'd be put to work with ninnies and idjits. Not ninnies and idjits!'

'There! What did I tell you?' said Jock, with a grin. 'He's always calling the other men that, so we just have to let him work right away from them. Still, he's right – most of the men here don't know the first thing about work on a farm. I wish my stepfather would let us have a few proper workers instead of these men.'

'Where's your stepfather?' said Julian, thinking he must be a bit odd to pour money into a little moorland farm like this, and yet choose the wrong kind of workers.

'He's away for the day,' said Jock. 'Thankfully!' he added, with a sideways look at the others.

'Why? Don't you like him?' asked Dick.

'He's all right,' said Jock. 'But he's not a farmer, though he makes out he's always wanted to be – and he doesn't like me one bit. I try to like him for Mum's sake. But I'm always glad when he's out of the way.'

'Your mum's nice,' said George.

'Oh, yes – Mum's great,' said Jock. 'You don't know what it means to her to have a little farm of her own again, and to be able to run it with the proper machinery and all.'

They came to a large barn. The door was locked.

'I told you what was in here before,' said Jock. 'Lorries! You can look through that hole here at them. Don't know why my stepfather wanted to buy so many, but I suppose he got them cheap – he loves to get things cheap and sell them for a profit! He did say they'd be useful on the farm, to take goods to the market.'

'Yes – you told us that when we were here yesterday,' said Dick. 'But you've got lots of wagons for that!'

'Yes. I reckon they weren't bought for the farm at all, but for holding here till prices go high and he can make a lot of money,' said Jock, lowering his voice. 'I don't tell Mum that. As long as she gets what she wants for the farm, I'm going to hold my tongue.'

The children were very interested in all this. They wished they could see Mr Andrews. He must be a strange man, they thought. Anne tried to imagine what he was like.

'Big and tall and dark and frowny,' she thought. 'Frightening and impatient, and he won't like children. People like that never do.'

They spent a very happy morning looking around the little farm. They went back to see Biddy the collie and her pups. Timmy stood patiently outside the shed, with his tail down. He didn't like George to take so much interest in other dogs.

A bell rang loudly.

'Good! Lunch!' said Jock. 'We'd better wash. We're all filthy. Hope you feel hungry, because I bet Mum's got a huge lunch for us.'

'I'm starving,' said Anne. 'It seems ages since we had breakfast. I've almost forgotten it!'

They all felt the same. They went into the farmhouse and were surprised to find a very nice little bathroom to wash in. Mrs Andrews was there, putting out a clean towel.

'Lovely little bathroom, isn't it?' she said. 'My husband had it put in for me. First new bathroom I've ever had!'

A delicious smell rose up from the kitchen downstairs.

'Come on!' said Jock, grabbing the soap. 'Let's hurry. We'll be down in a minute, Mum!'

And they were. Nobody was going to dawdle over washing when a big meal lay waiting for them downstairs!

7 Mr Andrews comes home

They all sat down to lunch. There was a big meat pie, a cold ham, salad, potatoes in their jackets, and home-made pickles. It was difficult to know what to choose.

'Have some of everything,' said Mrs Andrews, cutting the meat pie. 'Begin with the pie and go on to the ham. That's the best of living on a farm, you know – you do get plenty to eat.'

After the first course there were plums and thick cream, or jam tarts and the same cream. Everyone tucked in hungrily.

'I've never had such a lovely lunch in my life,' said Anne, at last. 'I wish I could eat some more but I can't. It was wonderful, Mrs Andrews.'

'Fantastic,' said Dick. That was his favourite word these holidays. 'Absolutely fantastic.'

'Woof,' said Timmy, agreeing. He'd had a plateful of meaty bones, biscuits and gravy, and he'd licked up every crumb and every drop. Now he wanted to have a snooze in the sun and not do a thing for the rest of the day.

The children felt a bit like that, too. Mrs Andrews handed them a chocolate each and sent them outside.

'You go and have a rest now,' she said. 'Talk to Jock. He doesn't get enough company of his own age in the holidays. You can stay for tea, if you like.'

'Oh thanks,' said everyone, although they all felt that they wouldn't even be able to manage a biscuit. But it was so nice at the farm that they felt they'd like to stay as long as they could.

'May we borrow one of Biddy's puppies to have with us?' asked Anne.

'If Biddy doesn't mind,' said Mrs Andrews, beginning to clear away. 'And if Timmy doesn't eat it up!'

'Timmy wouldn't dream of it!' said George at once. 'You go and get the puppy, Anne. We'll find a nice place in the sun.'

Anne went off to get the puppy. Biddy didn't seem to mind a bit. Anne cuddled the fat little thing against her, and went off to the others, feeling very happy. The boys had found a place

against a haystack, and sat leaning against it, the
sun shining down warmly on them.

'Those men of yours seem to take a long lunch,'
said Julian, not seeing any of them about.

Jock gave a snort. 'They're just lazy. I'd sack
them if I were my stepfather. Mum's told him how
badly the men work, but he doesn't say a word to
them. I've given up bothering. I don't pay their
wages – if I did, I'd sack the whole lot!'

'Let's ask Jock about the spook-trains,' said
George, fondling Timmy's ears. 'It'd be fun to
talk about them.'

'Spook-trains? Whatever are they?' asked
Jock, his eyes wide with surprise. 'Never heard
of them!'

'Haven't you?' asked Dick. 'Well, you don't
live very far from them, Jock!'

'Tell me about them,' said Jock. 'Spook-trains
– no, I've never heard of one of those.'

'Well, I'll tell you what we know,' said Julian.
'Actually we thought you'd be able to tell us
about them.'

He began to tell Jock about their visit to the
deserted railway yard, and Wooden-Leg Sam, and
his strange behaviour. Jock listened, enthralled.

'I wish I'd been with you! Let's all go there together, shall we?' he said. 'That was quite an adventure you had, wasn't it? I've never had a single adventure in all my life, not even a little one. Have you?'

The four children looked at one another, and Timmy looked at George. Adventures! What didn't they know about them? They'd had so many.

'Yes. We've had a lot of adventures – real ones – fantastic ones,' said Dick. 'We've been down in dungeons, we've been lost in caves, we've found secret passages, we've looked for treasure – well, I can't tell you what we've done! It'd take too long.'

'No it wouldn't,' said Jock eagerly. 'Please tell me. Go on. Did you all have the adventures? Little Anne, too?'

'Yes, all of us,' said George. 'And Timmy as well. He's rescued us from danger lots of times. Haven't you, Tim?'

'Woof, woof,' said Timmy, and thumped his tail against the hay.

They began to tell Jock about their many adventures. He was a very, very good listener. His eyes almost fell out of his head, and he went brick-red whenever they came to an exciting part.

'That's wonderful!' he said at last. 'I've never heard such things in my life before. Aren't you lucky? You just go around having adventures all the time, don't you? Hey – do you think you'll have one here, these holidays?'

Julian laughed. 'No. What kind of adventure would there be on these lonely moorlands? You've lived here for three years, and haven't even had a tiny adventure.'

Jock sighed. 'That's true. I haven't.' Then his eyes brightened again. 'But what about those spook-trains you were talking about? Perhaps you'll have an adventure with those?'

'Oh, no, I don't want to,' said Anne, in a horrified voice. 'An adventure with spook-trains would be horrible.'

'I'd like to go down to that old railway yard with you and see Wooden-Leg Sam,' said Jock longingly. 'That'd be a real adventure to me, you know – just talking to a funny old man like that, and wondering if he was suddenly going to throw things at us. Take me with you next time you go.'

'Well – I don't think that we planned to go again,' said Julian. 'There's nothing in his story except imagination – he's confused in the head through being alone there so much, guarding a yard where nothing and nobody ever comes. He's just remembering the trains that used to go in and out before they stopped using the line.'

'But the shepherd said the same as Sam,' said Jock. 'How about going down there one night and watching for a spook-train!'

'NO!' said Anne, in horror.

'You needn't come,' said Jock.

'I'll come,' said George at once. 'I'm not going to be left out. Timmy's coming, too.'

'Oh, please don't make these plans,' begged poor Anne. 'You'll make an adventure come, if you go on like this.'

Nobody took any notice of her. Julian looked at Jock's excited face.

'Well,' he said, 'if we do go there again, we'll tell you. And if we think we'll go watching for spook-trains, we'll take you with us.'

Jock looked as if he could hug Julian.

'That'd be great,' he said. 'Thanks so much. Spook-trains! Just imagine if we really did see one!

Who'd be driving it? Where would it come from?'

'Out of the tunnel, Wooden-Leg Sam says,' said Dick. 'But I don't see how we'd spot it, except by the noise it made, because apparently the spook-trains only arrive in the middle of the night. Never in the daytime. We wouldn't *see* much, even if we were there.'

It was such an exciting subject to Jock that he persisted in talking about it all afternoon. Anne got tired of listening, and went to sleep with Biddy's puppy in her arms. Timmy curled up by George and went to sleep too. He wanted to go for a walk, but he could see that there was no hope with all this talking going on.

It was tea-time before any of them had expected it. The bell rang, and Jock looked very surprised.

'Tea! Would you believe it? It's been so exciting talking about all this. And listen, if you don't decide to go spook-train hunting I'll go off by myself. If only I could have an adventure like the kind you've had, I'd be happy.'

They went in to tea, after waking Anne up with difficulty. She took the puppy back to Biddy, who received it gladly and licked it all over.

Julian was surprised to find that he was hungry again.

'Well,' he said, as he sat down at the table, 'I didn't think I'd feel hungry again for a week – but I do. What a wonderful tea, Mrs Andrews. Isn't Jock lucky to have meals like this always!'

There were home-made scones with new honey. There were slices of bread thickly spread with butter, and fresh cream cheese to go with it. There was sticky brown gingerbread, hot from the oven, and a big solid fruit cake that looked almost like a plum pudding when it was cut, it was so black.

'I wish I hadn't had so much lunch,' sighed Anne. 'I don't feel hungry enough to eat a bit of everything and I'd really like to!'

Mrs Andrews laughed. 'You eat what you can, and I'll give you some to take away, too,' she said. 'You can have some cream cheese, and the scones and honey – and some of the bread I made this morning. And maybe you'd like a slab of the gingerbread. I made plenty.'

'Oh, thanks,' said Julian. 'We'll be all right tomorrow with all that. You're a wonderful cook, Mrs Andrews. I wish I lived on your farm.'

There was the sound of a car coming slowly up

the rough track to the farmhouse, and Mrs Andrews looked up.

'That's Mr Andrews come back,' she said. 'My husband, you know, Jock's stepfather.'

Julian thought she looked a little worried. Perhaps Mr Andrews didn't like children and wouldn't be pleased to see them sitting around his table when he came home tired.

'Would you like us to go, Mrs Andrews?' he asked politely. 'Perhaps Mr Andrews would like a bit of peace for his meal when he comes in – and we're a bit of a crowd, aren't we?'

Jock's mother shook her head. 'No, you can stay. I'll get him a meal in the other room if he'd like it.'

Mr Andrews came in. He wasn't anything like Anne or the others had imagined him to be. He was a short, dark little man, with a weak face and a nose much too big for it. He looked harassed and bad-tempered, and stopped short when he saw the five children.

'Hello, dear,' said Mrs Andrews. 'Jock's got his friends here today. Would you like a bit of tea in your room? I can easily put a tray there.'

'Well,' said Mr Andrews, smiling a watery kind

of smile, 'perhaps it'd be best. I've had a worrying kind of day, and not much to eat.'

'I'll get you a tray of ham and pickles and bread,' said his wife. 'It won't take a minute. You go and wash.'

Mr Andrews went out. Anne was surprised that he seemed so small and looked a bit stupid. She'd imagined someone big and strong and clever, who was always doing important deals and making a lot of money. Well, he must be cleverer than he looked, to make enough money to give Mrs Andrews all she needed for her farm.

Mrs Andrews bustled around, laying a tray with a snow-white cloth and plates of food. Mr Andrews could be heard in the bathroom, splashing as he washed. Then he came downstairs and put his head in at the door.

'My meal ready?' he asked. 'Well, Jock – had a good day?'

'Yes, thanks,' said Jock, as his stepfather took the tray from his mother and turned to go. 'We went all around the farm this morning – and we talked and talked this afternoon. And oh – do you know anything about spook-trains?'

Mr Andrews was just going out of the door. He

turned in surprise. 'Spook-trains? What are you talking about?'

'Well, Julian says there's an old deserted railway yard a good way from here, and spook-trains are supposed to come out of the tunnel there in the dark of night,' said Jock. 'Have you heard of them?'

Mr Andrews stood stock still, his eyes on his stepson. He looked upset and shocked. Then he came back into the room and kicked the door shut behind him.

'I'll have my tea here after all,' he said. 'Well, to think you've heard of those spook-trains! I've been careful not to mention them to your mum or to you, Jock, for fear of scaring you!'

'Oh!' said Dick. 'Are they really true then? They can't be.'

'You tell me all you know, and how you know about it,' said Mr Andrews, sitting down at the table with his tray. 'Go on. Don't miss out a thing. I want to hear everything.'

Julian hesitated. 'There's nothing really to tell, sir – just a lot of nonsense.'

'You tell it me!' almost shouted Mr Andrews. 'Then I'll tell *you* a few things. And you won't

go near that old railway yard again – no, that
you won't!'

8 A lazy evening

The five children and Mrs Andrews stared in surprise at Mr Andrews when he shouted at them. He repeated some of his words again.

'Go on! You tell me all you know. And then I'll tell *you*!'

Julian decided to tell, very shortly, what had happened at the old railway yard, and what Wooden-Leg Sam had said. He made the tale sound rather boring. Mr Andrews listened to it with the greatest interest, never once taking his eyes off Julian.

Then he sat back and drank a whole cup of strong tea in one gulp. The children waited for him to speak, wondering what he had to say.

'Now,' he said, making his voice sound important and impressive, 'you listen to me. Don't any of you ever go down to that yard again. It's a bad place.'

'Why?' asked Julian. 'What do you mean

– a bad place?'

'Things happened there – years and years ago,' said Mr Andrews. 'Bad things. Accidents. It was all shut up after that and the tunnel wasn't used any more. Nobody was allowed to go there, and nobody did, because they were scared. They knew it was a bad place, where bad things happen.'

Anne felt frightened. 'But Mr Andrews – you don't mean there really are spook-trains, do you?' she asked, her face pale.

Mr Andrews pursed up his lips and nodded very solemnly indeed. 'That's exactly what I mean. Spook-trains come and go. Nobody knows why. But it's bad luck to be there when they come. They might take you away.'

Julian laughed. 'It's not as bad as that, surely! Anyway, you're frightening Anne, so let's change the subject. I don't believe in spook-trains.'

But Mr Andrews didn't seem to want to stop talking about the trains.

'Wooden-Leg Sam is right to hide himself when they come along,' he said. 'I don't know how he manages to stay on in a bad place like that. Never knowing when a train is going to come creeping out of that tunnel in the darkness.'

Julian wasn't going to have Anne frightened any more. He got up from the table and turned to Mrs Andrews.

'Thank you very much for a lovely day and lovely food!' he said. 'We must go now.'

'Wait a minute,' said Mr Andrews. 'I just want to warn you all very solemnly that you mustn't go down to that railway yard. You hear me, Jock? You might never come back. Old Wooden-Leg Sam's mad, and no wonder, with spook-trains coming along in the dead of night. It's a bad and dangerous place. You're not to go near it!'

'Well – thank you for the warning, Mr Andrews,' said Julian, politely, suddenly disliking the small man with the big nose very much indeed. 'We'll be going. Goodbye, Mrs Andrews. Goodbye, Jock. Come along tomorrow and have a picnic with us, will you?'

'Oh, thanks! Yes, I will,' said Jock. 'But wait a minute – aren't you going to take any food with you?'

'Yes, of course they are,' said Mrs Andrews, getting up from her chair.

She'd been listening to the conversation with a

look of puzzled wonder on her face. She went into the big, cold larder. Julian followed her. He carried the two baskets.

'I'll give you plenty,' said Mrs Andrews, putting loaves, butter and cream cheese into the baskets. 'I know what appetites you youngsters get. Now don't you be too scared at what my husband's just been saying – I saw that little Anne was frightened. I've never heard of the spook-trains, and I've been here for three years. I don't reckon there's much in the tale, you know, for all my husband's so set on warning you not to go down to the yard.'

Julian said nothing. He thought that Mr Andrews had behaved very oddly about the whole story. Was he the kind of person who believed in all sorts of silly things and got scared himself? He looked weak enough! Julian found himself wondering how a nice woman like Mrs Andrews could have married such a silly man.

Julian thanked Mrs Andrews, and insisted on paying her, though she'd have given him the food for nothing. She came into the kitchen with him and he saw that the others had already gone outside. Only Mr Andrews was left, eating ham and pickles.

'Goodbye, sir,' said Julian politely.

'Goodbye. And you remember what I've told you, boy,' said Mr Andrews. 'Bad luck comes to people who see the spook-trains – yes, terrible bad luck. You keep away from them.'

Julian gave a polite smile and went out. It was evening now and the sun was setting behind the moorland hills, though it still had a long way to go before it disappeared. He caught up with the others. Jock was with them.

'I'm just coming halfway with you,' said Jock. 'My stepfather was pretty scary about those trains, wasn't he?'

'I felt pretty scary too, when he was warning us about them,' said Anne. 'I won't go down to that yard again, ever. Will you, George?'

'If the boys did, I would,' said George, who didn't look very much as if she wanted to, all the same.

'*Are* you going to the yard again?' asked Jock, eagerly. 'I'm not scared. Not a bit. It'd be an adventure to go and watch for a spook-train.'

'We might go,' said Julian. 'We'll take you with us, if we do. But the girls can't come.'

'As if you could leave me behind!' said George angrily. 'When have I ever been scared of anything? I'm as brave as any of you.'

'Yes. I know. You can come as soon as we find out it's all a silly story,' said Julian.

'I'll come whenever you go,' flashed back George. 'Don't you dare to leave me out. I'll never speak to you again if you do.'

Jock looked very surprised at this sudden flare-up of temper from George. He didn't know how fierce she could be!

'I don't see why George shouldn't come,' he said.

But Julian wouldn't change his mind.

'I mean what I say. The girls can't come if we do go. Anne wouldn't want to come, and if George came without her she'd be left all alone up at the camp. She wouldn't like that.'

'She'd have Mr Luffy's company,' said George, looking sulky again.

'Idiot! As if we'd tell Mr Luffy we were going off exploring deserted railway yards watched over by a mad watchman who believes in spook-trains!' said Julian. 'He'd stop us going. You know what grown-ups are like. Or he'd come with us, which would be worse.'

'Yes. He'd see moths all the time, not spook-trains,' said Dick, with a grin.

'I'd better go back now,' said Jock. 'It's been a fun day. I'll come up tomorrow and picnic with you. See you.'

They called goodbye to Jock, and went on their way to the camp. It was nice to see it again, waiting for them, the two tents flapping a little in the breeze. Anne pushed her way through the tent-flap, wanting to check that everything was untouched.

Inside the tent it was very hot. Anne decided to put the food they'd brought under the bottom of the big gorse bush. It'd be cooler there. She was soon busy doing her little jobs. The others went down to see if Mr Luffy was back, but he wasn't.

'Anne! We're going to swim in the stream!' they called. 'We feel hot and dirty. Are you coming?'

'No, I won't come,' Anne called back. 'I've got lots of things to do.'

The others grinned at one another. Anne loved 'playing house'. So they left her to it, and went to the stream, from which yells and howls and shrieks soon came. The water was colder than they expected, and nobody liked to lie down in it – but everyone was well and truly splashed, and the icy-cold drops falling on their hot bodies made them squeal and yell. Timmy didn't mind the iciness of the water. He rolled over and over in it, enjoying himself.

'Look at him, showing off!' said Dick. 'Aha, Timmy, if I could swim in a fur coat like you, I wouldn't mind the cold water either.'

'Woof,' said Timmy, and climbed up the shallow bank. He shook himself violently and thousands of icy-cold silvery drops flew from him and landed on the three shivering children. They yelled and chased him away.

It was a pleasant, lazy evening. Mr Luffy didn't appear at all. Anne got a light meal of bread and cream cheese and a piece of gingerbread. Nobody felt like facing another big meal that day. They lay in the heather and talked comfortably.

'This is the kind of holiday I like,' said Dick.

'So do I,' said Anne. 'Except for the spook-trains. That's spoilt it a bit for me.'

'Don't be silly, Anne,' said George. 'If they're not real it's just a silly story, and if they're real, well, it might be an adventure.'

There was a little silence.

'Are we going down to the yard again?' asked Dick lazily.

'Yes, I think so,' said Julian. 'I'm not going to be scared off it by strange warnings from Pa Andrews.'

'Then let's go one night and wait to see if a spook-train does come along,' said Dick.

'I'll come too,' said George.

'No, you won't,' said Julian. 'You'll stay with Anne.'

George said nothing, but everyone could feel mutiny in the air.

'Do we tell Mr Luffy, or don't we?' said Dick.

'You know we've said we wouldn't,' said Julian. He yawned. 'I'm getting sleepy. And the sun has gone, so it'll soon be dark. I wonder where Mr Luffy is?'

'Do you think I'd better wait up and see if he wants something to eat?' said Anne, anxiously.

'No. Not unless you want to keep awake till midnight!' said Julian. 'He'll have got some food down in his tent. He'll be all right. I'm going to turn in. Coming, Dick?'

The boys were soon in their sleeping bags. The girls lay in the heather for a little while longer, listening to the lonely-sounding cry of the curlews going home in the dusk. Then they, too, went into their own tent.

Once safely in their sleeping bags, the two boys felt suddenly wide awake. They began to talk in low voices.

'Shall we take Jock down to see the yard in the daytime? Or shall we go one night and watch for the Train from Nowhere?' said Julian.

'Let's go and watch at night,' said Dick. 'We'll never see a spook-train in the daytime. Wooden-Leg Sam is interesting, especially when he chucks things about – but I don't like him enough to go and visit him again!'

'Well – if Jock wants to go and have a snoop around tomorrow morning when he comes, we'd better take him,' said Julian. 'We can always go one night, too, if we want to.'

'Right. We'll wait and see what Jock says,' said Dick.

They talked a little longer and then felt sleepy. Dick was just dropping off when he heard something coming wriggling through the heather.

A head was stuck through the opening of the tent.

'If you dare to come in, I'll smack your silly face,' said Dick, thinking it was Timmy. 'I know what you want, you pest – you want to flop down on my tummy. You just turn yourself around and go away!'

The head in the opening moved a little but didn't go away. Dick raised himself up on one elbow.

'Put one paw inside my tent and you'll be sent rolling down the hill!' he said. 'I love you very much in the daytime, but I'm not fond of you at night – not when I'm in a sleeping bag anyway. Scoot!'

The head made a strange apologetic sound. Then it spoke. 'Er – you're awake, I see. Are all of you all right? I'm only just back.'

'It's Mr Luffy,' said Dick, filled with horror. 'I'm so sorry! I thought you were Timmy, come to flop himself down on top of me, like he often does. I'm really sorry, sir.'

'Don't mention it!' said the shadowy head with a chuckle. 'Glad you're all right. See you tomorrow!'

9 Night visitor

Mr Luffy slept very late the next morning and nobody liked to disturb him. The girls yelled with laughter when they heard how Dick had spoken to him the night before, thinking he was Timmy the dog.

'He was very good about it,' said Dick. 'Seemed to think it was quite funny. I hope he'll still think so this morning!'

They were all sitting eating their breakfast – ham, tomatoes, and the bread Mrs Andrews had given them the day before. Timmy collected the bits as usual, and wondered if George would let him have a lick of the cream cheese she was now putting on her bread. Timmy loved cheese. He looked at it in the dish and sighed all over George. He could easily eat that in one mouthful!

'I wonder what time Jock will come up,' said George. 'If he came up pretty soon, we could go for a nice long walk over the moors, and picnic somewhere. Jock ought to know some great walks.'

'Yes. We'll mess about till he comes, and then tell him he's going to be our guide and take us on the nicest walk he knows,' said Anne. 'Oh Timmy! You've taken my nice lump of cream cheese right out of my fingers!'

'Well, you were waving it about under his nose, so what could you expect?' said George. 'He thought you were giving it to him.'

'Well, he can't have any more. It's too precious,' said Anne. 'Oh, dear – I wish we didn't eat so much. We keep bringing in stacks of food, and it hardly lasts any time.'

'I bet Jock will bring some more,' said Dick. 'Did you get a look into that enormous larder of his mum's? It's like a big cave, goes right back into the wall, with dozens of stone shelves – and all filled with food.'

'Is that Jock whistling?' said Anne.

It wasn't. It was a curlew, very high up.

'Too early for him yet,' said Julian.

After they'd cleared up, the boys went down to Mr Luffy's tent. He was awake, sitting at the entrance, eating some kind of breakfast. He waved a sandwich at them.

'Hello! I'm late this morning. I had a job getting back. I went much too far. Sorry I woke you up last night, Dick.'

'You didn't. I wasn't asleep,' said Dick, going red. 'Did you have a good day, Mr Luffy?'

'Bit disappointing. Didn't find all the creatures I'd hoped,' said Mr Luffy. 'What about you? Did you have a good day?'

'Great,' said Dick, and described it. Mr Luffy seemed very interested in everything, even in Mr Andrews's frightening warning about the railway yard.

'Silly man,' said Mr Luffy, shaking the crumbs off his front. 'All the same – I'd keep away from the yard, if I were you. Stories don't get about for nothing, you know. No smoke without fire!'

'Surely *you* don't think there's anything spooky about the trains there?' said Dick, in surprise.

'Oh, no – I doubt if there *are* any trains,' said Mr Luffy. 'But when a place has got a bad name it's usually best to keep away from it.'

Dick and Julian hastily changed the subject, afraid that Mr Luffy, like Mr Andrews, might also be going to forbid them to visit the railway yard. And the more they were warned about it and forbidden to go, the more they felt that they really must!

'We have to get back,' said Dick. 'We're expecting Jock – that's the boy from the farm – to come up for the day, and we thought we'd go out walking and take our food with us. Are you going out, too, sir?'

'Not today,' said Mr Luffy. 'My legs are tired and stiff with so much scrambling about yesterday, and I want to mount some of the specimens I found. Also I'd like to meet your farm friend – what's his name – Jock?'

'Yes,' said Julian. 'Right. We'll bring him along as soon as he comes, then off we'll go. You'll be left in peace all day!'

But Jock didn't come. The children waited for him all morning and he didn't turn up. They held up their lunch until they were too hungry to wait any longer, and then they had it on the heather in front of their tents.

'Funny,' said Julian. 'He knows where the camp is, because we pointed it out to him when he came halfway home with us yesterday. Perhaps he'll come this afternoon.'

But he didn't come in the afternoon either, nor

did he come after tea. Julian wondered whether or not to go and see what was up, but decided against it. There must be a good reason why Jock hadn't come, and Mrs Andrews wouldn't want them all visiting her two days running.

It was a disappointing day. They didn't like to leave the tents and go for even a short stroll in case Jock came. Mr Luffy was busy all day long with his specimens. He was sorry Jock had disappointed them.

'He'll come tomorrow,' he said. 'Have you got enough food? There's some in that tin over there if you want it.'

'Oh, no thanks,' said Julian. 'We've got plenty really. We're going to have a game of cards. Like to join us?'

'Yes, I think I will,' said Mr Luffy, getting up and stretching himself. 'Can you play rummy?'

They could – and they beat Mr Luffy because he couldn't play at all. He blamed his luck on his bad cards, but he enjoyed the game very much. He said the only thing that really put him off was the way that Timmy stood behind him and breathed down his neck all the time.

'I kept feeling certain that Timmy thought he

knew how to play my cards better than I could,' he complained. 'And whenever I did something wrong, he breathed down my neck harder than usual.'

Everyone laughed, and George privately thought that Timmy would probably play much better than Mr Luffy if only he could hold the cards.

Jock didn't come at all. They put the cards away when they could no longer see them, and Mr Luffy announced that he was going to bed.

'It was very late when I got back last night,' he said. 'I really must have an early night.'

The others decided to go to bed too. The thought of their cosy sleeping bags was always a nice one when darkness came on.

The girls crept into their bags and Timmy flopped down on George. The boys were in their bags about the same time and Dick gave a loud yawn.

'Goodnight, Ju,' he said, and fell fast asleep.

Julian was soon asleep too. In fact, everyone was sound asleep when Timmy gave a little growl. It was such a small growl that neither of the girls heard it, and certainly Dick and Julian didn't, away in their tent.

Timmy raised his head and listened intently.

Then he gave another small growl. He listened again. Finally he got up, shook himself, still without waking George, and stalked out of the tent, his ears pricked and his tail up. He'd heard somebody or something, and although he thought it was all right, he was going to make sure.

Dick was sound asleep when he felt something brushing against the outside of his tent. He awoke at once and sat up. He looked at the tent opening. A shadow appeared there and looked in.

Was it Timmy? Was it Mr Luffy? He mustn't make a mistake this time. He waited for the shadow to speak. But it didn't! It just stayed there as if it were listening for some movement inside the tent. Dick didn't like it.

'Timmy!' he said at last, in a low voice.

Then the shadow spoke: 'Dick? Or is it Julian? It's Jock here. I've got Timmy beside me. Can I come in?'

'*Jock*!' said Dick, in surprise. 'What have you come at this time of night for? And why didn't you come today? We waited ages for you.'

'Yes, I know. I'm really sorry,' said Jock's voice, and the boy wriggled himself into the tent.

Dick poked Julian awake. 'Julian! Here's Jock

– and Timmy. Get off me, Timmy.'

'I'm really sorry I didn't come today,' said Jock, 'but my stepfather suddenly announced he wanted me to go somewhere with him for the whole day. Can't think why. He doesn't bother about me as a rule.'

'That was mean of him, seeing that he knew you were planning to come on a picnic with us,' said Julian. 'Was it something important?'

'No. Not at all,' said Jock. 'He drove off to Endersfield – that's about forty miles away – parked me in the public library there, saying he'd be back in a few minutes – and he didn't come back till past tea-time! I had some sandwiches with me, luckily. I felt really angry about it.'

'Never mind. Come tomorrow instead,' said Dick.

'I can't,' said Jock in despair. 'He's gone and arranged for me to meet the son of some friend of his – a boy called Cecil Dearlove – what a name! I've got to spend the day with this awful boy. The worst of it is Mum's quite pleased about it. She never thinks my stepfather takes enough notice of me – good thing he doesn't, I think.'

'Oh no – so you won't be able to come

tomorrow either,' said Julian. 'Well – what about the next day?'

'It should be all right,' said Jock. 'But I have a feeling I'll have the dear love of a Cecil plonked on me for the day – to show him the cows and the puppies. Ugh! When I could be with you four and Timmy.'

'It's really annoying,' said Julian.

'I thought I'd better come and tell you,' said Jock. 'It's the first chance I've had, creeping up here tonight. I've brought some more food for you, by the way. I guessed you'd want some. I feel so disappointed about that adventure – you know, going to see the railway yard. I was going to ask you to take me today.'

'Well – if you can't come tomorrow either – and perhaps not the next day – what about going one night?' said Dick. 'Would you like to come up tomorrow night, about this time? We won't tell the girls. We'll just go off by ourselves, we three boys – and watch!'

Jock was too thrilled to say a word. He let out a deep breath of joy. Dick laughed.

'Don't get too excited. We probably won't see a thing. Bring a torch if you've got one. Come to our tent and jerk my toe. I'll probably be awake, but if I'm not, that'll wake me up! And don't say a word to anyone of course.'

'Of course not,' said Jock, overjoyed. 'Well – I suppose I'd better be going. It was strange coming over the moorland in the dark. There's no moon, and the stars don't give much light. I've left the food outside the tent. Better look out that Timmy doesn't get it.'

'Right. Thanks,' said Julian.

Jock went backwards out of the tent, with Timmy obligingly licking his nose all the way. Jock then found the bag of food and rolled it in to Julian, who put it safely under the groundsheet.

'Goodnight,' said Jock, in a low voice, and they heard him scrambling over the heather.

Timmy went with him, pleased at this unexpected visitor, and the chance of a midnight walk. Jock was glad to have the dog's company. Timmy went right to the farm with him and then bounded back over the moorland to the camping place, longing to pounce on the rabbits he could smell here and there, but wanting to get back to George.

* * *

In the morning Anne was amazed to find the food in her 'larder' under the gorse bush. Julian had put it there to surprise her.

'Look at this!' she cried, in astonishment. 'Meat pies – more tomatoes – eggs, where did they come from?'

'Spook-train brought them in the night,' said Dick, with a grin.

'Volcano shot them up into the air,' said Mr Luffy, who was also there.

Anne threw a tea towel at him.

'Tell me how it came here,' she demanded. 'I was worried about what to have for breakfast – and now there's more than we can possibly eat. Who put it there? George, do you know?'

But George didn't. She glanced at the smiling faces of the two boys.

'I bet Jock was here last night,' she said to them. 'Wasn't he?' And to herself she said: 'Yes – and somehow I think they've planned something together. You won't trick *me*, Dick and Julian. I'll be on the lookout from now on! Wherever you go, I go too!'

10 *Hunt for a spook-train*

That day passed pleasantly enough. The children, Timmy and Mr Luffy all went off to a pool high up on the moorlands. It was called 'the Green Pool' because of its cucumber-green colour. Mr Luffy explained that some chemicals found there caused the water to look green.

'I hope we won't come out looking green, too,' said Dick, getting into his swimming trunks. 'Are you going to swim, Mr Luffy?'

Mr Luffy was. The children expected him to be a bad swimmer and to splash about at the edge and do very little – but to their surprise he was really good in the water, and could swim faster even than Julian.

They had great fun, and when they were tired they came out to sunbathe. The main road ran alongside the Green Pool, and the children watched a flock of sheep being driven along, then a car or two came by, and finally a big lorry. A boy sat beside the driver, and to the children's surprise he waved wildly at them.

'Who was that?' said Julian, astonished.

George's sharp eyes had seen who it was. 'It was Jock! Sitting beside the driver. And, look, here comes his stepfather's shiny new car. Jock decided to go with the lorry-driver instead of his stepfather! I don't blame him!'

The bright new car came by, driven by Mr Andrews. He didn't glance at the children by the wayside, but drove steadily on after the lorry.

'Going to market, I suppose,' said Dick, lying back again. 'Wonder what they're taking?'

'So do I,' said Mr Luffy. 'He must sell his farm produce at very high prices to be able to buy that car and all the machinery and gear you've told me about. Clever man, Mr Andrews!'

'He doesn't look at all clever,' said Anne. 'He looks a bit weak, really. I can't imagine him being clever enough to haggle with anyone at the market, or get the better of them.'

'Very interesting,' said Mr Luffy. 'Well, what about another dip before we have our lunch?'

It was a very nice day, and Mr Luffy was very good company. He could make good jokes while keeping a very straight face, and only the fact that his ear waggled violently showed the others that he was enjoying the joke. His right ear seemed to love to join in the joke, even if Mr Luffy's face was as solemn as Timmy's.

They arrived home at the camp about tea-time and everyone helped to get tea ready. They took it down to eat in front of Mr Luffy's tent. As the evening came on Julian and Dick felt excitement rising in them. In the daytime neither of them really believed a word about the spook-trains, but as the sun sank and long shadows crept down the hills they felt a thrill. Would they see anything exciting that night?

It was a very dark night at first, because clouds lay across the sky and hid even the stars. The boys said goodnight to the girls and snuggled down into their sleeping bags. They watched the sky through the tent opening.

Gradually the big clouds thinned out. A few stars appeared. The clouds thinned still more and fled away in rags. Soon the whole sky was bright with pinpoints of light, and a hundred thousand stars looked down on the moorlands.

'We'll have a bit of starlight to see by,' whispered

Julian. 'That's good. I don't want to stumble about over the heather and break my ankle in rabbit-holes in the dark. But I don't want to use my torch on the way to the yard in case it's seen.'

'It's going to be fun!' Dick whispered back. 'I hope Jock comes. It'll be annoying if he doesn't.'

He did come. There was a scrambling over the heather and once again a shadow appeared at the tent opening.

'Julian! Dick! I've come. Are you ready?'

It was Jock's voice, of course. Dick's thumb pressed the switch of his torch and for a moment its light fell on Jock's red, excited face, and then was switched off again.

'Hello, Jock! You made it!' said Dick. 'Was that you in the lorry this morning, going by the Green Pool?'

'Yes. Did you see me? I saw you and waved like mad,' said Jock. 'I wanted to stop the lorry and get down and speak to you, but the driver's really bad-tempered. He wouldn't stop. Said my stepfather would be angry with him if he did. Did you see *him* – my stepfather, I mean? He was in his car behind.'

'Were you off to market or something?' asked Julian.

'I expect that's where the lorry was going,' said Jock. 'It was empty, so I suppose my stepfather was going to pick up something there. I came back in the car. The lorry was supposed to come later.'

'How was Cecil Dearlove?' asked Dick, grinning in the darkness.

'Awful! Worse than his name,' groaned Jock. 'Wanted to play soldiers all the time! The worst thing is I've got to have him at the farm for the day tomorrow. Another day wasted. What shall I do with him?'

'Roll him in the pigsty,' suggested Dick. 'Or put him with Biddy's puppies and let him sleep there. Tell him to play soldiers with them.'

Jock chuckled. 'I wish I could. But Mum is really pleased that my stepfather's got this Cecil boy for me to be friends with. Let's not talk about it. Are you ready to start off?'

'Yes,' said Julian, and began to scramble quietly out of his bag. 'We didn't tell the girls. Anne doesn't want to come, and I don't want George to leave Anne by herself. Now, let's be very, very quiet till we're out of hearing.'

Dick got out of his bag too. The boys hadn't undressed that night, except for their coats, so all they had to do was to slip these on, and then crawl out of the tent.

'Which is the way – over there?' whispered Jock.

Julian took his arm and guided him. He hoped he wouldn't lose his way in the starlit darkness. The moorland looked so different at night!

'If we head for that hill you can dimly see over there against the sky, we should be going in the right direction,' said Julian.

So on they went, keeping towards the dark hill that rose up to the west.

It seemed much farther to the railway yard at night than in the daytime. The three boys stumbled along, sometimes almost falling as their feet caught in tufts of heather. They were glad when they found a path they could keep on.

'This is about where we met the shepherd,' said Dick, in a low voice. He didn't know why he spoke so quietly. He just felt as if he should. 'I'm sure we can't be very far off now.'

They went on for some way, and then Julian

pulled Dick by the arm.

'Look,' he said. 'Down there, I think that's the old yard. You can see the lines gleaming faintly here and there.'

They stood on the heathery slope above the old yard, straining their eyes. Soon they could make out dim shapes. Yes, it was the railway yard.

Jock clutched Julian's sleeve. 'Look – there's a light down there! Do you see it?'

The boys looked – and sure enough, down in the yard towards the other side of it, was a small yellow light. They stared at it.

'Oh – I think I know what it is,' said Dick, at last. 'It's the light in the watchman's little hut. Don't you think so, Ju?'

'Yes. You're right,' said Julian. 'I tell you what we'll do – we'll creep right down into the yard, and go over to the hut. We'll look inside and see if Wooden-Leg Sam is there. Then we'll hide somewhere and wait for the spook-train to come!'

They crept down the slope. Their eyes had got used to the starlight by now, and they were beginning to see fairly well. They got right down to the yard, where their feet made a noise.

They stopped. 'Someone will hear us if we make a row like this,' whispered Julian.

'Who will?' whispered back Dick. 'There's no one here except Sam in his hut!'

'How do you know there isn't?' said Julian. 'Jock, don't make such a racket with your feet!'

They stood there, debating what was the best thing to do.

'We'd better walk right around the edge of the yard,' said Julian at last. 'As far as I remember, the grass has grown there. We'll walk on that.'

So they made their way to the edge of the yard. Sure enough, there was grass there, and they walked on it without a sound. They went slowly and softly to where the light shone dimly in Sam's little hut.

The window was high and small. It was just about at the level of their heads, and the three boys cautiously eased themselves along to it and looked in.

Wooden-Leg Sam was there. He sat sprawled in a chair, smoking a pipe. He was reading a newspaper, squinting painfully as he did so. He obviously hadn't had his broken glasses mended yet. On a chair beside him was his wooden leg.

He'd unstrapped it, and there it lay.

'He's not expecting the spook-train tonight, or he wouldn't have taken off his wooden leg,' whispered Dick.

The light flickered and shadows jumped about the tiny hut. It was a poor, badly furnished little place, dirty and untidy. A cup without saucer or handle stood on the table, and a tin kettle boiled on a rusty stove.

Sam put down his paper and rubbed his eyes. He muttered something. The boys couldn't hear it, but they felt certain it was something about his broken glasses.

'Are there many lines in this yard?' whispered Jock, tired of looking in at Sam. 'Where do they go to?'

'There's a tunnel about half a mile or so up there,' said Julian, pointing past Jock. 'The lines come from there, and then break up into pairs – for shunting and so on, in the old days, I suppose, when this place was used.'

'Let's go up the lines to the tunnel,' said Jock. 'Come on. There's nothing to see here. Let's walk up to the tunnel.'

'All right,' said Julian. 'We might as well. I don't

expect we'll see much up there either! I think these spook-trains are all in Sam's imagination!'

They left the little hut with its lonely light, and made their way around the yard again. Then they followed the single-track line away from the yard and up towards the tunnel. They walked along, talking in low voices.

And then things began to happen! A far-off muffled noise came rumbling out of the tunnel, which was now so near that the boys could see its black mouth. Julian heard it first. He stood still and clutched Dick.

'Listen! Can you hear that?'

The others listened.

'Yes,' said Dick. 'But it's only a train going through one of the underground tunnels – the noise is echoing out through this one.'

'It isn't. That noise is made by a train coming through this tunnel!' said Julian.

The noise grew louder and louder. A clanking could be heard too. The boys stepped off the lines and crouched together by the side, waiting, hardly daring to breathe.

Could it be the spook-train? They watched for lights to appear like fiery eyes in the tunnel. But none came. It was darker than night in there! But the noise came nearer and nearer and nearer. Could there be the noise of a train without a train? Julian's heart began to beat twice as fast, and Dick and Jock found themselves clutching one another without knowing it.

The noise grew thunderous, and then out from the tunnel came something long and black, with a faint glow in front that passed quickly and was gone. The noise deafened the boys, and then the clanking and rumbling grew less as the train, or whatever it was, passed by. The ground trembled and then was still.

'Well, there you are,' said Julian, in a trembling voice. 'The spook-train – without a light or a signal! Where's it gone? To the yard, do you think?'

'Shall we go and see?' asked Dick. 'I didn't see anyone in the cab, but there must be *someone* driving it! How strange! It *sounded* real enough, anyway.'

'We'll go to the yard,' said Jock, who, of the three, seemed the least affected. 'Come on.'

They made their way very slowly – and then Dick gave a sharp cry. 'Ow! I've twisted my ankle. Just a minute!'

He sank down to the ground in great pain. It was only a sharp twist, not a sprain, but for a few minutes Dick could do nothing but groan. The others dared not leave him. Julian knelt by him, offering to rub the ankle, but Dick wouldn't let him touch it. Jock stood by anxiously.

It took about twenty minutes for Dick's ankle to be strong enough for him to stand on again. With the help of the others he got to his feet and tested his ankle. 'It's all right, I think. I can walk on it – slowly. Now we'll go to the yard and see what's happening!'

But as they started to walk slowly back, they heard a noise coming up the lines from the far-away yard. Rumble, rumble, rumble, jangle, clank!

'It's coming back again!' said Julian. 'Stand still. Watch! It'll be going back into the tunnel!'

They stood still and watched and listened. Again the noise came nearer and grew thunderous. They saw a glow, and then it passed. The train disappeared into the blackness of the tunnel mouth and they heard the echo of its rumblings for some time.

'Well, there you are! There *is* a spook-train!'

said Julian, trying to laugh, though he felt very shaken. 'It came and it went – where from or where to, nobody knows! But we've heard it and seen it, in the middle of the night. And very creepy it was, too!'

11 Mostly about Jock

The three boys stood close together in the darkness. They couldn't believe that they'd found what they'd come looking for so doubtfully! What kind of train was this that had come rumbling out of the tunnel so mysteriously, and then, after a pause at the yard, had gone just as mysteriously back again?

'If only I hadn't twisted my ankle, we could have followed the train down the lines to the yard, and have gone quite close to it there,' groaned Dick. 'What an idiot I am, messing things up at the most exciting moment!'

'You couldn't help it,' said Jock. 'We've seen the spook-train! I can hardly believe it. Does it go all by itself, with nobody to drive it? Is it a real train?'

'Judging by the noise it made, it's real all right,' said Julian. 'And it shot out smoke, too. It's really strange. I don't like it much.'

'Let's go and see what's happened to Wooden-Leg Sam,' said Dick. 'I bet he's under his bed!'

They made their way slowly back to the yard, Dick limping a little, although his ankle was practically all right again. When they came to the yard they looked towards Sam's hut. The light was no longer there.

'He's turned it off and got under the bed!' said Dick. 'Poor Sam! It must be terrifying for him. Let's go and look into his hut.'

They went over to it and tried to see in at the window. But there was nothing to be seen. The hut was in complete darkness. Then suddenly a little flare flashed out somewhere near the floor.

'Look – there's Sam! He's lighting a match,' said Julian. 'See – he's peering out from under the bed. He looks scared stiff. Let's tap on the window and ask him if he's all right.'

But that was the wrong thing to do! As soon as Julian tapped sharply on the window, Sam gave an anguished yell and disappeared under the bed again, his wavering match-light going out.

'It's come to take me!' they heard him wailing. 'It's come to take me! And me with my wooden leg off too.'

'We're frightening him,' said Dick. 'Come on. Let's leave him. He'll have a fit or something if we call out to him. He honestly thinks the spook-train's come to get him.'

They wandered around the dark yard for a few minutes, but there was nothing to find out in the darkness. No more rumbling came to their ears. The spook-train was evidently not going to run again that night.

'Let's go back,' said Julian. 'That was really exciting! Honestly, my hair stood on end when that train came puffing out of the tunnel. Where on earth did it come from? And what's the reason for it?'

They began to walk back to the camp. They scrambled through the heather, tired but excited.

'Shall we tell the girls we've seen the train?' said Dick.

'No,' said Julian. 'It'd only scare Anne, and George would be furious if she knew we'd gone without her. We'll wait and see if we discover anything else before we say anything to anyone.'

'Right,' said Dick. 'You'll hold your tongue, too, won't you, Jock?'

'Course,' said Jock, scornfully. 'Who would I tell? My stepfather? Not likely! He'd be furious if he knew we'd ignored his warnings and gone down to see the spook-train after all!'

He suddenly felt something warm against his legs, and gave a startled cry: 'What's this? Get away!'

But the warm thing turned out to be Timmy, who had come to meet three boys. He pressed against each of them in turn and whined a little.

'He says, "Why didn't you take me with you?"' said Dick. 'Sorry, Timmy, but we couldn't. George would never have spoken to us again if we'd taken you, and left her behind! How would you have liked spook-trains, Timmy? Would you have run into a corner somewhere and hidden?'

'Woof,' said Timmy, scornfully. As if he'd be afraid of anything!

They reached their camping place and began to speak in whispers. 'Goodbye, Jock. Come up tomorrow if you can. Hope you don't have that Cecil boy to cope with!'

'Goodbye! See you soon,' whispered Jock, and disappeared into the darkness, with Timmy at his heels. Another chance of a midnight walk? Good, thought Timmy, just what he'd like! It was hot in the tent, and a scamper in the cool night air would be lovely.

Timmy growled softly when they came near to Olly's Farm, and stood still, the hackles on his neck rising up a little. Jock put his hand on the dog's head and stopped.

'What's the matter, boy? Burglars or something?'

He strained his eyes in the darkness. Big clouds now covered the stars and there was no light at all to see by. Jock made out a dim light in one of the barns. He crept over to it to see what it was. It went out as he came near, and then he heard the sound of footsteps, the quiet closing of the barn door, and the click of a padlock as it was locked.

Jock crept nearer – too near, for whoever it was must have heard him and swung around, lashing out with his arm. He caught Jock on the shoulder, and the boy overbalanced. He almost fell, and the man who had struck him clutched hold of him. A torch was put on and he blinked in the sudden light.

'It's you, Jock!' said an astonished voice, rough and impatient. 'What are you doing out here at this time of night?'

'Well, what are *you* doing?' demanded Jock, wriggling free.

He switched on his own torch and let the light fall on the man who had caught him. It was Peters, one of the farm workers, the one in whose lorry he'd ridden earlier that day.

'What's it got to do with you?' said Peters, angrily. 'I had a breakdown, and I've only just got back. You're fully dressed! Where have you been at this time of night? Did you hear me come in and get up to see what was happening?'

'You never know!' said Jock cheekily. He wasn't going to say anything that might make Peters suspicious of him. 'You just never know!'

'Is that Biddy?' said Peters, seeing a dark shadow slinking away. 'Have you been out with Biddy? What on earth have you been doing?'

Jock thanked his lucky stars that Peters hadn't spotted it was Timmy, not Biddy. He moved off without saying another word. Let Peters think what he liked! It was bad luck, though, that Peters had had a breakdown and come in late. If the man told his stepfather he'd seen Jock up and dressed in the middle of the night, there'd be questions asked by both his mother and his stepfather, and Jock, who was a truthful boy, would find things very difficult to explain.

He scuttled off to bed, climbing up the pear-tree outside his window, and dropping quietly into his room. He opened his door softly to hear if anyone was awake in the house, but all was dark and silent.

'That horrible Peters!' thought Jock. 'If he tells on me, I'm in trouble!'

He got into bed, pondered over the events of the night for a few minutes, and then slid into an uneasy sleep, in which spook-trains, Peters and Timmy kept doing very strange things. He was glad to awake in the bright, sunny morning and find his mother shaking him.

'Get up, Jock! You're very late. What's made you so sleepy? We're halfway through breakfast!'

Peters, apparently, hadn't said anything to Jock's stepfather about seeing Jock in the night. Jock was very thankful. He began to plan how to slip off to the others at the camp. He'd take them some food! That'd be a good excuse.

'Mum, can I take a basket of stuff to the campers?' he said, after breakfast. 'They must be running short now.'

'Well, that boy is coming,' said his mother. 'What's his name – Cecil something? Your stepfather says he's a nice boy. You did enjoy your day with him yesterday, didn't you?'

Jock would have said quite a lot of uncomplimentary things about dear Cecil if his stepfather hadn't been there, sitting by the window reading the paper. As it was, he shrugged his shoulders and made a face, hoping that his mother would understand his feelings. She did.

'What time is Cecil coming?' she said. 'Perhaps there's time for you to run to the camp with a basket.'

'I don't want him running off up there,' said Mr Andrews, suddenly butting into the conversation, and putting down his newspaper. 'Cecil may be here at any minute – and I know what Jock's like! He'd start talking to those kids and forget all about coming back. Cecil's dad is a good friend of mine, and Jock's got to be polite to him, and be here to welcome him. There's to be no running off to that camp today.'

Jock looked sulky. Why was his stepfather suddenly interfering in his plans like this? Rushing him off to the town, making him take Cecil for a friend! Just when some other children had come into his lonely life and livened it up, too! It was really annoying.

'Perhaps I can go up to the camp myself with some food,' said his mother, comfortingly. 'Or maybe the children will come down for some.'

Jock was still sulky. He stalked out into the yard and went to look for Biddy. She was with her pups who were now trying to crawl around the shed after her. Jock hoped the campers would come to fetch food themselves that day. Then at least he'd get to talk to them.

Cecil arrived by car. He was about the same age as Jock, though he was small for twelve years old. He had longish curly hair and his clothes were very, very clean and well-ironed.

'Hello!' he called to Jock. 'What shall we play? Soldiers?'

'No. Gladiators,' said Jock, who had suddenly remembered his old gladiator costume. He rushed indoors, grinning, to change into it.

Cecil was wandering around by himself. To his horror, as he turned a corner, a terrifying figure rose up from behind a wall, gave a horrible yell and pounced on him, waving what looked like a dangerous axe.

Cecil turned and fled, howling loudly, with Jock leaping madly after him, whooping for all he was worth, and thoroughly enjoying himself. He'd had to play at soldiers all the day before with dear Cecil. He didn't see why Cecil shouldn't play what *he* wanted all day today!

Just at that moment, the four campers arrived to fetch food, with Timmy running beside them. They stopped in amazement at the sight of Cecil running like the wind, howling dismally, and a warrior leaping fiercely after him.

Jock saw them, did a comical war-dance all around them, much to Timmy's amazement, yelled dramatically, pretended to cut off Timmy's tail and then raced after the vanishing Cecil.

The children began to laugh helplessly.

'Oh!' said Anne, with tears of laughter in her eyes. 'That must be Cecil he's after. I expect this is Jock's revenge for having to play soldiers all day with him yesterday. Look, there they go around the pigsty. Poor Cecil. He really thinks he's going to be scalped!'

Cecil disappeared into the farm kitchen, sobbing, and Mrs Andrews ran to comfort him. Jock came back to the others, grinning all over his face.

'Hello,' he said. 'I'm just having a nice quiet game with dear Cecil. I'm so glad to see you. I wanted to come over, but my stepfather said I couldn't – I have to play with Cecil.'

'Will your mum be cross with you for frightening Cecil like that? Perhaps we'd better not ask her for any food yet?' said Julian.

'Yes, you'd better wait a bit,' said Jock, leading them to the sunny side of the haystack they'd rested by before. 'Hello, Timmy! Did you get back all right last night?'

Jock had completely forgotten that the girls didn't know about the events of the night before. Anne and George at once pricked up their ears. Julian frowned at Jock, and Dick gave him a secret nudge.

'What's up?' said George, seeing all this. 'What happened last night?'

'Oh, I just came up to have a little night-talk with the boys – and Timmy walked back with me,' said Jock, airily. 'Hope you didn't mind him coming, George.'

George flushed an angry red. 'You're keeping something from me,' she said to the boys. 'Yes, you are. I know you are. I think you went off to the railway yard last night! Did you?'

There was an awkward silence. Julian shot an annoyed look at poor Jock, who could have kicked himself.

'Go on – tell me,' persisted George, an angry frown on her forehead. 'You're so mean! You did go! And you never woke me up to go with you! I think you're horrible!'

'Did you see anything?' said Anne, her eyes going from one boy to another.

Each of the girls sensed that there had been some kind of adventure in the night.

'Well,' began Julian. And then there was an interruption. Cecil came around the haystack, his eyes red with crying. He glared at Jock.

'Your dad wants you,' he said. 'You're horrible, and I want to go home. Can't you hear your dad yelling for you? He's really angry – but

I'm not sorry for you! I hope he grounds you for a month!'

12 George loses her temper

Jock made a face at Cecil and got up. He went slowly off around the haystack, and the others listened in silence for angry voices. But none came.

'He frightened me,' said Cecil, sitting down by the others.

'Poor ickle ting,' said Dick at once.

'Darling baby,' said George.

'Mummy's boy,' said Julian.

Cecil glared at them all. He got up again, very red.

'If I didn't know my manners, I'd smack your faces,' he said, and marched off hurriedly, before his own could be smacked.

The four sat in silence. They were sorry for Jock. George was angry and sulky because she knew the others had gone off without her the night before. Anne was worried.

They all sat there for about ten minutes. Then around the haystack came Jock's mother, looking upset. She was carrying a big basket of food.

The children all stood up politely. 'Good morning, Mrs Andrews,' said Julian.

'I'm sorry I can't ask you to stay today,' said Mrs Andrews. 'But Jock has really behaved very foolishly. I've sent him up to bed for the day. You won't be able to see him, I'm afraid. Here's some food for you to take. I'm really very sorry about all this. I can't think what came over Jock to behave in such a way. It's not like him.'

Cecil's face appeared around the haystack, looking smug. Julian grinned to himself.

'Would you like us to take Cecil for a nice long walk over the moors?' he said. 'We can climb hills and jump over streams and scramble through the heather. It'd make such a nice day for him.'

Cecil's face immediately disappeared.

'Well,' said Mrs Andrews, 'that'd be very kind of you. Now that Jock's been sent upstairs for the day there's no one for Cecil to play with. But I'm afraid he's a bit of a nervous boy, you know. You'll have to go carefully with him. Cecil! Cecil! Where are you? Come and make friends with these children.'

But Cecil had gone. There was no answer at

all. He didn't want to make friends with 'these children'. He knew better than that! Mrs Andrews went in search of him, but he'd completely disappeared.

The four children weren't surprised. Julian, Dick and Anne grinned at one another. George stood with her back to them, still sulky.

Mrs Andrews came back again, out of breath.

'I can't find him,' she said. 'Never mind. I'll find something for him to do when he appears again.'

'Yes. Perhaps you've got a colouring book and wax crayons? Or a nice easy jigsaw puzzle to do?' said Julian, very politely.

The others giggled. A smile appeared on Mrs Andrews's face.

'Naughty boy!' she said. 'Oh dear – poor Jock. Well it's his own fault. Now goodbye, I must get on with my work.'

She hurried off to the dairy. The children looked around the haystack. Mr Andrews was getting into his car. He'd soon be gone. They waited a few minutes till they heard the car set off down the rough cart-track.

'That's Jock's bedroom – where the pear tree

is,' said Julian. 'Let's just have a word with him before we go. It's a shame.'

They went across the farmyard and stood under the pear tree – all except George, who stayed behind the haystack with the food, frowning. Julian called up to the window above: 'Jock!'

A head came out. 'Hello! It's miserable being stuck up here on this sunny day. Where's dear Cecil?'

'I don't know. Probably in the darkest corner of one of the barns,' said Julian. 'Jock, if things are difficult in the daytime, come up at night. We've got to see you somehow.'

'Right,' said Jock. 'Where's George?'

'Sulking behind the haystack,' said Dick. 'We'll have a terrible day with her now. You let the cat right out of the bag, you idjit!'

'Yes. I'm a ninny and an idjit,' said Jock, and Anne giggled. 'Look – there's Cecil. Will you tell him to beware of the bull?'

'Is there a bull?' said Anne, looking alarmed.

'No. But that's no reason why he shouldn't watch out for one,' grinned Jock. 'See you! Have a nice day!'

The three left him, and strolled over to Cecil,

who had just appeared out of a dark little shed. He made a face at them, and stood ready to run to the dairy where Mrs Andrews was busy.

Julian suddenly clutched Dick and pointed behind Cecil.

'The bull! Beware of the bull!' he yelled suddenly.

Dick entered into the joke.

'The bull's loose! Look out! Beware of the bull!' he shouted.

Anne gave a shriek. It all sounded so real that, although she knew it was a joke, she felt half scared.

'The bull!' she cried.

Cecil turned green. His legs shook.

'W-w-w-where is it?' he stammered.

'Look out behind you!' yelled Julian, pointing.

Poor Cecil, convinced that a large bull was about to pounce on him from behind, gave a wail and ran on tottering legs to the dairy. He threw himself against Mrs Andrews.

'Save me, save me! The bull's chasing me.'

'But there's no bull here,' said Mrs Andrews, in surprise. 'Honestly, Cecil! Was it a pig after you, or something?'

Helpless with laughter, the three children made their way back to George. They tried to tell her about the make-believe bull, but she turned away and wouldn't listen. Julian shrugged his shoulders. Best to leave George to herself when she was in one of her rages! She didn't lose her temper as often as she used to, but when she did she was very difficult indeed.

They went back to the camp with the basket of food. Timmy followed soberly. He knew something was wrong with George and he was unhappy. His tail was down, and he looked miserable. George wouldn't even pat him.

When they got back to the camp, George flared up.

'How could you go off without me when I told you I wanted to come? How could you take Jock and not let me go? I think you're absolutely horrible. I never really thought you'd do a thing like that, you and Dick.'

'Don't be silly, George,' said Julian. 'I told you that you had to stay with Anne. I'll tell you exactly what happened – it's really exciting!'

'What? Tell me quickly!' begged Anne, but George obstinately turned away her head as if she wasn't interested.

Julian began to relate all the strange events of the night. Anne listened breathlessly. George was listening too, although she pretended not to. She was very angry and very hurt.

'Well, that's it,' said Julian, when he'd finished. 'If that's what people mean by spook-trains, there was definitely one puffing in and out of that tunnel! It was really scary. Sorry you weren't there too, George – but I didn't want to leave Anne alone.'

George wasn't accepting any apologies. She still looked furious.

'I suppose Timmy went with you,' she said. 'I think that was mean of him – to go without waking me, when he knew I'd like to be with you on the adventure.'

'Oh, don't be so silly,' said Dick, in disgust. 'It's ridiculous to be angry with Tim, too! You're making him miserable. And anyway, he *didn't* come with us. He just came to meet us when we got back, and then went off to keep Jock company on his way back to the farm.'

'Oh,' said George, and she reached out her hand to pat Timmy, who was filled with delight.

'At least Timmy was loyal to me then. That's something.'

There was a silence. Nobody ever knew quite how to treat George when she was in one of her moods. It was really best to leave her alone, but they couldn't very well go off and leave the camp just because George was there, cross and sulky.

Anne took hold of George's arm. She was miserable when George behaved like this.

'George,' she began, 'there's no need to be cross with me, too. *I* haven't done anything!'

'If you weren't such a little coward, too afraid to go with us, I'd have been able to go too,' said George unkindly, dragging her arm away.

Julian was annoyed. He saw Anne's hurt face and was angry with George.

'Quiet, George,' he said. 'You're being horrible, saying nasty things like that! I'm surprised at you.'

George was ashamed of herself, but she was too proud to say so. She glared at Julian.

'And *I'm* surprised at *you*,' she said. 'After all the adventures we've had together, you try to keep me out of this one. But you *will* let me come next time, won't you, Julian?'

'What! After the way you've behaved?' said

Julian, who could be just as stubborn as George when he wanted to. 'No chance. This is my adventure and Dick's – and perhaps Jock's. Not yours or Anne's.'

He got up and stalked down the hill with Dick. George sat pulling bits of heather off the stems, looking mutinous and angry. Anne blinked back tears. She hated this sort of thing. She got up to get lunch ready. Perhaps after a good meal they would all feel better.

Mr Luffy was sitting outside his tent, reading. He'd already seen the children that morning. He looked up, smiling.

'Hello! Come to talk to me?'

'Yes,' said Julian, an idea uncurling itself in his mind. 'Could I have a look at that map of yours, Mr Luffy? The big one you've got showing every mile of these moorlands?'

'Of course. It's in the tent somewhere,' said Mr Luffy.

The boys found it and opened it. Dick at once guessed why Julian wanted it. Mr Luffy went on reading.

'It shows the railways that run under the moorlands too, doesn't it?' said Julian.

Mr Luffy nodded. 'Yes. There are quite a few lines. I suppose it was easier to tunnel under the moors from valley to valley than make a permanent way over the top of them. In any case, a railway over the moors would probably be completely covered by snow in the winter.'

The boys bent their heads over the big map; it showed the railways as dotted lines when they went underground, but as long black lines when they appeared in the open air, in the various valleys.

They found exactly where they were. Then Julian's finger ran down the map a little and came to where a small line showed itself at the end of a dotted line.

He looked at Dick, who nodded. Yes – that showed where the tunnel was, out of which the spook-train had come, and the lines to the deserted yard. Julian's finger went back from the yard to the tunnel, where the dotted lines began. His finger traced the dotted lines a little way till they became whole lines again. That was where the train came out into another valley!

Then his finger showed where the tunnel that led from the yard appeared to join up with another one, that also ran for some distance before coming out into yet another valley. The boys looked at one another in silence.

Mr Luffy suddenly spotted a day-flying moth and got up to follow it. The boys took the chance of talking to one another.

'The spook-train either runs through its own tunnel to the valley beyond – or it turns off into this fork and runs along to the other valley,' said Julian, in a low voice. 'I tell you what we'll do, Dick. We'll get Mr Luffy to run us down to the nearest town to buy something – and we'll go to the station there and ask a few questions about these two tunnels. We may find out something.'

'Good idea,' said Dick, as Mr Luffy came back. 'Sir, are you very busy today? Could you possibly run us down to the nearest town after lunch?'

'Certainly, certainly,' said Mr Luffy.

The boys looked at one another in delight. *Now* they might find out something! But they wouldn't take George with them. No – they would punish her for her bad temper by leaving her behind!

13 A thrilling plan

Anne called them to lunch.

'Come on!' she cried. 'I've got it all ready. Tell Mr Luffy there's plenty for him, too.'

Mr Luffy came along willingly. He looked approvingly at the spread set out on a white cloth on the ground.

'Hmm! Salad. Hard-boiled eggs. Slices of ham. And what's this – apple-pie! Don't tell me you cooked that here, Anne.'

Anne laughed. 'No. All this came from the farm, of course. Except the lime cordial and water.'

George ate with the others, but said hardly a word. She was sulking, and Mr Luffy looked at her several times, puzzled.

'Are you all right, George?' he said, suddenly.

George went red.

'Yes, thank you,' she said, and tried to be more herself, although she couldn't raise a smile at all. Mr Luffy watched her, and was relieved to see that she ate as much as the others. Probably had some sort of argument, he guessed correctly. Well, it'd blow over! He knew better than to interfere.

They finished lunch and drank all the lime cordial and water. It was a hot day and they were very thirsty indeed. Timmy emptied all his dish of water and went and gazed longingly into the bucket of washing-water. But he was too well-behaved to drink it, now that he knew he mustn't. Anne laughed, and poured some more water into his dish.

'Well,' said Mr Luffy, beginning to fill his old brown pipe, 'if anyone wants to come into town with me this afternoon, I'll be starting in fifteen minutes.'

'I'll come!' said Anne, at once. 'Will you come too, George?'

'No,' said George, and the boys heaved a sigh of relief. They'd guessed she wouldn't want to come with them – but, if she'd known what they were going to try and find out, she'd definitely have come!

'I'm going for a walk with Timmy,' said George, when all the washing up had been done.

'All right,' said Anne, who secretly thought that

George would be much better left on her own to work off her bad temper that afternoon. 'See you later.'

George and Timmy set off. The others went with Mr Luffy to where his car was parked beside the great rock. They got in.

'The trailer's still attached to it,' called Julian. 'Wait a minute. Let me get out and undo it. We don't want to take an empty trailer bumping along behind us for miles.'

'I always forget to undo the trailer,' said Mr Luffy. 'The times I take it along without meaning to!'

The children winked at one another. Luffy was always doing things like that. No wonder his wife fussed around him like an old hen with one foolish chicken when he was at home.

They went off in the car, jolting over the rough road till they came to the smooth highway. They stopped in the centre of the town. Mr Luffy said he'd meet them for tea at five o'clock at the hotel opposite the car park.

The three of them set off together, leaving Mr Luffy to go to the library and browse there. It seemed funny to be without George. Anne didn't like it, and said so.

'Well, we don't like going off without George either,' said Julian. 'But honestly, she can't behave like that and get away with it. I thought she'd grown out of that sort of thing.'

'You know how she loves adventures,' said Anne. 'If I hadn't felt so scared you'd have taken me along, and George would have gone too. It's true what she said about me being a coward.'

'You're not,' said Dick. 'You can't help being scared of things sometimes – after all, you're the youngest of us – but being scared doesn't make you a coward. I've known you to be as brave as any of us when you've been scared stiff!'

'Where are we going?' asked Anne. The boys told her, and her eyes sparkled.

'Are we going to find out where the spook-train comes from? It might come from one of two valleys then, judging from the map.'

'Yes. The tunnels aren't really very long ones,' said Julian. 'Not more than a mile, I should think. We thought we'd ask at the station and see if anyone knows anything about the old railway yard and the tunnel beyond. We won't say a word about the spook-train of course.'

They walked into the station. They went up to a railway plan and studied it. It didn't tell them much. Julian turned to a young station assistant who was wheeling a trolley along.

'Excuse me, could you help us? We're camping up on the moorlands, and we're quite near a deserted railway yard with lines that run into an old tunnel. Why isn't the yard used any more?'

'Don't know,' said the young man. 'You should ask old Tucky there – see him? He knows all the tunnels under the moors like the back of his hand. Worked in them all when he was a boy.'

'Thanks,' said Dick, pleased. They went over to where the station assistant was sitting in the sun, enjoying a rest.

'Excuse me,' said Julian politely. 'I've been told that you know all about the moorland tunnels like the back of your hand. They must be very, very interesting.'

'My father and my grandfather built those tunnels,' said the old man, looking up at the children out of small faded eyes that watered in the strong sunlight. 'And I've been guard on all the trains that ran through them.'

He mumbled a long string of names, going

through all the list of tunnels in his mind. The children waited patiently till he'd finished.

'There's a tunnel near where we're camping on the moorlands,' said Julian, getting a word in at last. 'We're not far from Olly's Farm. We came across an old deserted railway yard, with lines that led into a tunnel. Do you know it?'

'Oh yes, that's an old tunnel,' said Tucky, nodding his grey head, on which his cap sat all crooked. 'Hasn't been used for many a long year. Nor the yard either. Wasn't enough traffic there, far as I remember. They shut up the yard. Tunnel isn't used any more.'

The boys exchanged glances. So it wasn't used any more! Well, they knew better.

'The tunnel joins another, doesn't it?' said Julian.

Tucky, pleased at their interest in the old tunnels he knew so well, got up and went into an office behind. He came out with a dirty, much-used map, which he spread out on his knee. His black fingernail pointed to a mark on the map.

'That's the yard, see? It was called Olly's Yard, after the farm. There're the lines to the tunnel. Here's the tunnel. It runs right through to Kilty

Vale – there it is. And here's where it used to join the tunnel to Roker's Vale. But that was bricked up years ago. Something happened there – the roof fell in, I think it was – and the company decided not to use the tunnel to Roker's Vale at all.'

The children listened with the utmost interest. Julian worked it out in his mind. If that spook-train came from anywhere then it must come from Kilty Vale, because that was the only place the lines went to now, since the way to Roker's Vale had been bricked up where the tunnels joined.

'I suppose no trains run through the tunnel from Kilty Vale to Olly's Yard now, then?' he said.

Tucky snorted. 'Didn't I tell you it hasn't been used for years? The yard at Kilty Vale's been turned into something else, though the lines are still there. There's been no engine through that tunnel since I was a young man.'

This was all very, very interesting. Julian thanked Tucky so much that he wanted to tell the children everything all over again. He even gave them the old map.

'Oh, thanks,' said Julian, delighted to have it.

He looked at the others. 'This'll be really useful!' he said, and they nodded.

They left the pleased old man and went out into the town. They found a little park and sat down on a seat. They were longing to discuss all that Tucky had told them.

'It's really strange,' said Dick. 'No trains run there now – the tunnel's not been used for ages – and Olly's Yard must have been derelict for years.'

'And yet, there appear to be trains that come and go!' said Julian.

'Then they *must* be spook-trains,' said Anne, her eyes wide and puzzled. 'Julian, they must be, mustn't they?'

'Looks like it,' said Julian. 'It's very mysterious. I can't understand it.'

'Ju,' said Dick, suddenly. 'I know what we'll do! We'll wait one night again till we see the spook-train come out of the tunnel to the yard. Then one of us can sprint off to the *other* end of the tunnel – it's only about a mile long – and wait for it to come out the other side! Then we'll find out why a train still runs from Kilty Vale to Olly's Yard through that old tunnel.'

'Good idea,' said Julian, thrilled. 'What about tonight? If Jock comes, he can go, too. If he doesn't, just you and I will go. *Not* George.'

They all felt excited. Anne wondered if she'd be brave enough to go too, but she knew that when the night came she wouldn't feel half as brave as she did now! No, she wouldn't go. There was really no need for her to join in this adventure at present. It hadn't even turned out to be a proper one yet – it was only an unsolved mystery!

George hadn't come back from her walk when they reached the camp. They waited for her, and at last she appeared with Timmy, looking tired out.

'Sorry I was an idiot this morning,' she said at once. 'I've walked my temper off! Don't know what came over me.'

'That's all right,' said Julian. 'Forget it.'

They were all very glad that George had recovered her temper, for she was a very prickly person indeed when she was angry. She was quiet and said nothing at all about spook-trains or tunnels. So they said nothing either.

The night was clear. Stars shone out brilliantly again in the sky. The children said goodnight to

Mr Luffy at ten o'clock and got into their sleeping bags. Julian and Dick didn't plan to go exploring till midnight, so they lay and talked quietly.

About eleven o'clock they heard somebody moving cautiously outside. They wondered if it was Jock, but he did not call out to them. Who could it be?

Then Julian saw a familiar head outlined against the starlit sky. It was George. But what on earth was she doing? He couldn't work it out. Whatever it was she wasn't making any noise over it, and she obviously thought the boys were asleep. Julian gave a nice little snore or two just to let her go on thinking so.

At last she disappeared. Julian waited a few minutes and then put his head cautiously out of the tent opening. He felt about, and his fingers brushed against some string. He grinned to himself and got back into the tent.

'I've found out what George was doing,' he whispered. 'She's put string across the entrance of our tent, and I bet it runs to her tent and she's tied it to her big toe or something, so that if we go out without her she'll feel the pull of the string when we go through it and wake up and follow us!'

'Good old George,' chuckled Dick. 'Well, she'll be unlucky. We'll squeeze out under the sides of the tent!'

Which was what they did at about a minute past twelve! They didn't disturb George's string at all. They were out on the heather and away down the slope while George was sleeping soundly in her tent beside Anne, waiting for the pull on her toe which didn't come. Poor George!

The boys arrived at the deserted railway yard and looked to see if Wooden-Leg Sam's light was on. It was. So the spook-train hadn't come along *that* night, yet.

They were just scrambling down to the yard when they heard the train coming. There was the same rumbling noise as before, muffled by the tunnel – and then out of the tunnel, again with no lights, came the spook-train, clanking on its way to the yard!

'Quick, Dick! Sprint off to the tunnel opening and watch for the train to go back in again. And I'll find my way across the moor to the other end of the tunnel. There was a path marked on that old map, and I'll follow that!' Julian's words tumbled over each other in his excitement. 'I'll watch for the spook-train to complete its journey, and see if it vanishes into thin air or what!'

And off he went to find the path that led over the moors to the other end of the tunnel. He meant to see what happened at the other end if he had to run all the way!

14 Jock comes to camp

Julian found the path by chance and went along it as fast as he could. He used his torch, for he didn't think he'd meet anyone out on such a lonely way at that time of night. The path was very overgrown, but he could follow it fairly easily, even running at times.

'If that spook-train stops about twenty minutes in the yard again, as it did before, it'll give me just enough time to reach the other end of the tunnel,' panted Julian. 'I'll be at Kilty's Yard before it comes.'

It seemed a very long way. But at last the path led downwards, and some way below him Julian could see what might be a railway yard. Then he saw that big sheds were built there – or what looked like big sheds in the starlight.

He remembered what the station assistant had said. Kilty's Yard was used for something else now – maybe the lines had been taken up. Maybe even the tunnel had been blocked up, too. He slipped quickly down the path and came into what had once been the old railway yard. Big buildings loomed up on every side. Julian thought they must be workshops of some kind. He switched his torch on and off very quickly, but the short flash had shown him what he was looking for – two pairs of railway lines. They were old and rusty, but he knew they must lead to the tunnel.

He followed them closely, right up to the black mouth of the dark tunnel. He couldn't see inside at all. He switched his torch on and off quickly. Yes – the lines led right inside the tunnel. Julian stopped and wondered what to do.

'I'll sneak into the tunnel a little way and see if it's bricked up anywhere,' he thought. So in he went, walking between one pair of lines. He put on his torch, sure that no one would see its light and ask him what he was doing out so late at night.

The tunnel stretched before him, a great yawning hole, disappearing into deep blackness. It wasn't bricked up. Julian saw a little niche in the brickwork of the tunnel and decided to crouch in it. It was one of the niches made for workmen to stand in when trains went by in the old days.

Julian crouched down in the dirty old niche and waited. He glanced at the luminous face of his watch. He'd been twenty minutes getting here. Maybe the train would be along in a few minutes. He'd be very, very close to it! Julian couldn't help wishing that Dick was with him. It was so creepy waiting there in the dark for a mysterious train that apparently belonged to no one and came and went from nowhere to nowhere!

He waited and he waited. Once he thought he heard a rumble far away down the tunnel, and he held his breath, feeling certain that the train was coming. But it didn't come. Julian waited for half an hour and still the train hadn't appeared. What had happened to it?

'I'll wait another ten minutes and then I'm going,' Julian decided. 'I've had enough of hiding in a dark, dirty tunnel waiting for a train that doesn't come! Maybe it's decided to stay in Olly's Yard for the night.'

After ten minutes he gave up. He left the tunnel, went into Kilty's Yard and then up the path to the moors. He hurried along it, eager to see if Dick was at the other end of the tunnel. Surely he'd wait there till Julian came back!

Dick was there, tired and impatient. When he saw a quick flash from Julian's torch he answered it with his own. The two boys joined company thankfully.

'You've been *ages*!' said Dick. 'What happened? The spook-train went back into the tunnel ages and ages ago. It only stayed about twenty minutes in the yard again.'

'Went back into the tunnel!' exclaimed Julian. 'Did it really? Well, it never came out the other side! I waited for ages. I never even heard it – although I did hear a very faint rumble once, or thought I did.'

The boys fell silent, puzzled and mystified. What sort of a train was this that puffed out of a tunnel at dead of night, and went back again, but didn't appear out of the other end?

'I suppose the entrance to that second tunnel the station assistant told us about *is* really bricked up?' said Julian at last. 'If it wasn't, the train could go down there, of course.'

'Yes. That's the only solution, if the train's a real one and not a spook one,' agreed Dick. 'Well, we can't go exploring the tunnels now – let's wait and do it in the daytime. I've had enough tonight!'

Julian had had enough too. In silence the two boys went back to camp. They forgot about the string in front of their tent, and scrambled right through it. They got into the sleeping bags thankfully.

The string, fastened to George's big toe through a hole she'd cut in her sleeping bag, pulled hard, and George woke up with a jump. Timmy was awake, having heard the boys come back. He licked George when she sat up.

George hadn't undressed properly. She slipped quickly out of her bag and crawled out of her tent. Now she'd catch the two boys going off secretly and follow them!

But there was no sign or sound of them anywhere around. She crawled silently to their tent. Both boys had fallen asleep immediately, tired out with their midnight trip. Julian snored a little, and Dick breathed so deeply that George could hear him as she crouched outside, listening. She was very puzzled. Someone had pulled at her toe – so somebody must have scrambled through that string. After listening for a few minutes, she gave up and went back to her tent.

In the morning, George was furious! Julian and Dick related their night's adventure, and George could hardly believe that once again they'd gone without her – and that they'd managed to get away without disturbing the string! Dick saw George's face and couldn't help laughing.

'Sorry, George. We discovered your trick and avoided it when we set out – but we forgot all about it coming back. We must have given your toe a real tug. Did we? I suppose you *did* tie the other end of the string to your toe?'

George looked as if she wanted to throw all the breakfast things at him. Fortunately for everyone Jock arrived at that moment. He didn't wear his usual beaming smile but seemed a bit subdued.

'Hello, Jock!' said Julian. 'Just in time for a bit of breakfast. Sit down and join us.'

'I can't,' said Jock. 'I've only got a few minutes. Listen, I've got some horrible news. I'm being sent away to stay with my stepfather's sister for two weeks! Two weeks! You'll be gone when I come back, won't you?'

'Yes. But, Jock, *why* have you got to go away?'

said Dick, surprised. 'Has there been an argument or something?'

'I don't know,' said Jock. 'Mum won't say, but she looks miserable. My stepfather's in a horrible temper. I think they want me out of the way for some reason. I don't know this sister of my stepfather's very well – only met her once – but she's not very nice.'

'Well, come over here and stay with us, if they want to get rid of you,' said Julian, sorry for Jock. Jock's face brightened.

'That's a great idea!' he said.

'Fantastic,' agreed Dick. 'I don't see what's to stop you. If they want to get rid of you, it can't matter where you go for a fortnight. We'd love to have you.'

'Right. I'll come,' said Jock. 'I won't say anything about it to my stepfather, though. I'll let Mum into the secret. She was going to take me away today, but I'll just tell her I'm coming to you instead. I don't think she'll tell on me, and hopefully she'll settle things with my step-aunt.'

Jock's face looked happy again now. The others smiled back, even George, and Timmy wagged his tail. It'd be nice to have Jock – and what a lot they had to tell him.

He went off to break the news to his mother, while the others washed up and cleared things away. George became sulky again when Jock was gone. She just could not or would not realise that Julian meant what he said!

When they began to discuss everything that had happened the night before, George refused to listen.

'I don't care about your stupid spook-trains any more,' she said. 'You wouldn't let me join you when I wanted to, and now I'm not interested.'

And she walked off with Timmy, not saying where she was going.

'Let her go,' said Julian, feeling cross. 'What does she expect me to do? Give in and say we'll let her come the next time we go?'

'We said we'd go in the daytime,' said Dick. 'She could come then, because if Anne doesn't want to come it won't matter leaving her here alone in the daytime.'

'You're right,' said Julian. 'Let's call her back and tell her.'

But by that time George was out of earshot.

'She's taken sandwiches,' said Anne. 'She means

to be gone all day. Isn't she silly?'

Jock came back after a time, with two warm rugs and an extra jumper and more food.

'It was hard work persuading Mum,' he said. 'But she said yes at last. Although I'd have come anyway! I'm not going to be pushed around by my stepfather just out of spite. Isn't this great! I never thought I'd be camping out with you. If there isn't room in your tent for me, Julian, I can sleep out on the heather.'

'There'll be room,' said Julian. 'Hello, Mr Luffy! You've been out early!'

Mr Luffy came up and glanced at Jock. 'Ah, is this your friend from the farm? How do you do? Come to spend a few days with us? I see you have an armful of rugs!'

'Yes. Jock's coming to camp a bit with us,' said Julian. 'Look at all the food he's brought. Enough to feed an army!'

'It is indeed,' said Mr Luffy. 'Well, I'm going to go through some of my specimens this morning. What are you going to do?'

'Oh, mess about till lunch-time,' said Julian. 'Then we might go for a walk.'

Mr Luffy went back to his tent and they could

hear him whistling softly as he set to work. Suddenly Jock sat up straight and looked alarmed.

'What's the matter?' asked Dick.

Then he heard what Jock had heard. A shrill whistle blown loudly some way off.

'That's my stepfather's whistle,' said Jock. 'He's whistling for me. Mum must have told him, or else he's found out I've come over here.'

'Quick – let's hide,' said Anne. 'If you're not here he can't take you back! Come on! Maybe he'll get tired of looking for you, and go.'

Nobody could think of a better idea, and certainly nobody wanted to face a furious Mr Andrews. All four shot down the slope and made their way to where the heather was high and thick. They burrowed into it and lay still, hidden by some high bracken.

Mr Andrews's voice could soon be heard, shouting for Jock, but no Jock appeared. Mr Andrews came out by Mr Luffy's tent. Mr Luffy, surprised at the shouting, put his head out of his tent to see what it was all about. He didn't like the look of Mr Andrews at all.

'Where's Jock?' Mr Andrews demanded, scowling at him.

'I really don't know,' said Mr Luffy.

'He's got to come back,' said Mr Andrews, roughly. 'I won't have him hanging about here with those kids.'

'What's wrong with them?' inquired Mr Luffy. 'I find them very well-behaved and polite.'

Mr Andrews stared at Mr Luffy, and put him down as a silly, harmless old man who would probably help him to get Jock back if he went about it the right way.

'Now listen,' said Mr Andrews. 'I don't know who you are, but you must be a friend of the children's. And if so, then I'd better warn you they're running into danger.'

'Really? In what way?' asked Mr Luffy, mildly and disbelievingly.

'There's bad and dangerous places about these moorlands,' said Mr Andrews. 'Very bad. I know them. And those children have been messing about in them. And if Jock comes here, he'll start messing about too, and I don't want him to get into any danger. It'd break his mother's heart.'

'Quite,' said Mr Luffy.

'Well, will you talk to him and send him back?' said Mr Andrews. 'That railway yard now – that's a very dangerous place. And people do say that there are spook-trains there. I wouldn't want Jock to be mixed up in anything like that.'

'Quite,' said Mr Luffy again, looking closely at Mr Andrews. 'You seem very concerned about this – er – railway yard.'

'Me? Oh, no,' said Mr Andrews. 'Never been near the horrible place. I wouldn't want to see spook-trains – make me run a mile! It's just that I don't want Jock to get into danger. I'd be grateful if you'd talk to him and send him home, when they all come back from wherever they are.'

'Quite,' said Mr Luffy again, very irritatingly.

Mr Andrews gazed at Mr Luffy's bland face and felt angry. 'Quite, quite, quite!' Gr-r-r-r-r-r!

He turned and went away. When he'd gone for some time, and was a small speck in the distance, Mr Luffy called loudly.

'He's gone! Please send Jock here so that I can – er – say a few words to him.'

Four children appeared from their heathery hiding place. Jock went over to Mr Luffy, looking mutinous.

'I just wanted to say,' said Mr Luffy, 'that I completely understand why you want to be away from your stepfather, and that I consider it's no business of mine where you go in order to get away from him!'

Jock grinned. 'Oh, thanks,' he said. 'I thought you were going to send me back!' He rushed over to the others. 'It's all right,' he said. 'I'm going to stay! How about going and exploring down that tunnel after lunch? We *might* find that spook-train then!'

'Good idea!' said Julian. 'We will! Poor old George – she'll miss this adventure too!'

15 George has an adventure

George had gone off with one fixed idea in her mind. She was going to find out something about that mysterious tunnel! She thought she'd walk over the moorlands to Kilty's Yard, and see what she could see there. Maybe she could walk right back through the tunnel itself!

She soon came to Olly's Yard. There it lay below her, with Wooden-Leg Sam pottering about. She went down to speak to him. He didn't see or hear her coming and jumped violently when she called to him.

He swung around, squinting at her fiercely.

'You clear off!' he shouted. 'I've been told to keep you children out of here, see? Do you want me to lose my job?'

'Who told you to keep us out?' asked George, puzzled as to who could have known they'd been in the yard.

'*He* did,' said the old man. He rubbed his eyes,

and then peered at George short-sightedly again. 'I've broken my glasses,' he said.

'Who's "he" – the person who told you to keep us out?' said George.

But the old watchman seemed to have one of his sudden strange changes of temper again. He bent down and picked up a large clod of earth. He was about to fling it at George when Timmy gave a loud and menacing growl. Sam dropped his arm.

'You clear out,' he said. 'You don't want to get a poor old man like me into trouble, do you? You look a nice kind boy, you do. You wouldn't get Wooden-Leg Sam into trouble, would you?'

George turned to go. She decided to take the path that led to the tunnel and look inside. But when she got there, there was nothing to see. She didn't feel that she wanted to walk all alone inside that dark mouth, so she took the path that Julian had taken the night before, over the top of the tunnel. But she left it halfway to look at a strange mound that jutted up from the heather just there.

She scraped away at the heather and found something hard beneath. She pulled at it but it wouldn't give. Timmy, thinking she was obligingly digging for rabbits, came to help. He scrambled below the heather – and then he suddenly gave a bark of fright and disappeared!

George screamed: 'Timmy! What have you done? Where are you?'

To her enormous relief she heard Timmy's bark some way down. Where *could* he be? She called again, and once more Timmy barked.

George tugged at the tufts of heather, and then suddenly she saw what the strange mound was. It was a built-up vent-hole for the old tunnel – a place where the smoke came curling out in the days when steam-trains ran there often. It had been barred across with iron, but the bars had rusted and fallen in, and heather had grown thickly over them.

'Oh, Timmy, you must have fallen down the vent,' said George, anxiously. 'But not very far down. Wait a bit and I'll see what I can do. If only the others were here to help!'

But they weren't, and George had to work all by herself to try and get down to the broken bars. It took her a very long time, but at last she had them exposed, and saw where Timmy had fallen down.

He kept giving short little barks, as if to say: 'It's all right. I can wait. I'm not hurt!'

George had to sit down and take a rest after her efforts. She was hungry, but she said to herself that she wouldn't eat till she'd somehow got down to Timmy, and found out where he was. Soon she began her task again.

She climbed down through the fallen-in vent. It was very difficult, and she was terrified of the rusty old iron bars breaking off under her weight. But they didn't.

Once down in the vent she discovered steps made of great iron nails projecting out. Some of them had thin rungs across. There had evidently once been a ladder up to the top of the vent. Most of the rungs had gone, but the iron nails that supported them still stood in the brick walls of the old round vent. She heard Timmy give a little bark. He was quite near her now.

Cautiously she went down the great hole. Her foot touched Timmy. He'd fallen on a collection of broken iron bars, which, caught in part of the old iron ladder, stuck out from it, and made a rough landing place for the dog to fall on.

'Oh, Timmy,' said George, horrified. 'How am

I going to get you out of here? This hole goes right down into the tunnel.'

She couldn't possibly pull Timmy up the hole. It was equally impossible to get him down. He could never climb down the iron ladder, especially as it had so many rungs missing.

George was in despair. 'Oh, Timmy! Why did I lose my temper and walk out on the others to do some exploring all by myself? Don't fall, Timmy. You'll break your legs if you do.'

Timmy had no intention of falling. He was frightened, but so far his strange landing place felt firm. He kept very still.

'Listen, Tim,' said George, at last. 'The only thing I can think of is to climb down around it somehow and see how far it is to the tunnel itself. There might even be someone there to help! No, that's silly. There can't be. But I might find an old rope – anything – that I could use to help you down with. What a nightmare!'

George gave Timmy a reassuring pat, and then began to feel about for the iron rungs with her feet. Further down they were all there, and it was easy to climb lower and lower. She was soon down in the tunnel itself. She had her torch with her and switched it on. Then she nearly gave a scream of horror.

Just near to her was a silent train! She could almost touch the engine. Was it – could it be – the spook-train itself? George stared at it, breathing fast.

It looked very, very old and out of date. It was smaller than the trains she was used to – the engine was smaller and so were the trucks. It had a long funnel and the wheels were different from those of ordinary trains. George stared at the silent train by the light of her torch, her mind in a muddle. She really didn't know *what* to think!

It *must* be the spook-train! It had come from this tunnel the night before, and had gone back again – and it hadn't run all the way through to Kilty's Yard, because Julian had watched for it, and it hadn't come out there. No – it had run here, to the middle of the dark tunnel, and there it stood, waiting for night so that it could run again.

George shivered. The train belonged to years and years ago! Who drove it at night? Did anybody? Or did it run along without a driver, remembering its old days and old ways? No, that

was silly. Trains didn't think or remember. George
shook herself and remembered Timmy.

And just at that very moment, poor Timmy lost
his foothold on the iron bars, and fell! He'd leaned
out to listen for George, his foot had slipped –
and now he was hurtling down the vent! He gave
a mournful howl.

He hit part of the ladder and that stopped his
headlong fall for a moment. But down he went
again, scrabbling as he fell, trying to get hold of
something to save himself.

George heard him howl and knew he was
falling. She was so horror-stricken that she
couldn't move. She stood there at the bottom of
the vent like a statue, not even breathing.

Timmy fell with a thump beside her, and a
groan was jerked out of him. In an instant George
was down by him on her knees. 'Timmy! Are you
hurt? Are you alive? Oh, Timmy, say something!'

'Woof,' said Timmy, and got up rather unsteadily
on his four legs. He'd fallen on a pile of the softest
soot! The smoke of many, many years had sooted
the walls of the vent, and the weather had sent it
down to the bottom, until a pile had collected at
one side. Timmy had fallen plump in the middle

of it, and almost buried himself. He shook himself violently, and soot flew out all over George.

She didn't know or care. She hugged him, and her face and clothes grew as black as soot! She felt about and found the soft pile that had saved Timmy from being hurt.

'It's soot! I came down the other side of the vent, so I didn't know the soot was there. Oh, Timmy, how lucky! I thought you'd be killed – or at least badly hurt,' said George.

He licked her sooty nose and didn't like the taste of it.

George stood up. She didn't like the idea of climbing up that horrible vent again – and, anyway, Timmy couldn't. The only thing to do was to walk out of the tunnel. She wouldn't have fancied walking through the tunnel before, in case she met the spook-train – but here it was, close beside her, and she'd been so worried about Timmy that she'd completely forgotten it.

Timmy went over to the engine and smelt the wheels. Then he jumped up into the driver's cab. Somehow the sight of Timmy doing that took away all George's fear. If Timmy could jump up into the spook-train, there couldn't be much for her to be afraid of!

She decided to examine the trucks. There were four of them, all covered. Shining her torch, she climbed up into one of them, pulling Timmy up behind her. She expected to find it empty, unloaded many, many years ago by long-forgotten railwaymen.

But it was loaded with boxes! George was surprised. Why did a spook-train run around with boxes in it? She shone her torch on to one – and then quickly switched it out!

She'd heard a noise in the tunnel. She crouched down in the truck, put her hand on Timmy's collar, and listened. Timmy listened, too, the hackles rising on his neck.

It was a clanging noise. Then there came a bang. Then a light shone out, and the tunnel was suddenly as bright as day!

The light came from a big lamp in the side of the tunnel. George peered cautiously out through a crack in the truck. She saw that this place must be where the tunnel forked. One fork went on to Kilty's Yard – but surely the other fork was supposed to be bricked up? George followed the lines with her eyes. One set went on down the

tunnel to Kilty's Yard, the other set ran straight
into a big wall, which was built across the second
tunnel that once led to Roker's Yard.

'It *is* bricked up, just as the station assistant
told Julian,' said George to herself. And then she
stared in amazement, clutching the side of the
truck, hardly believing her eyes.

Part of the wall was opening before her! Before
her very eyes, a great mass of it slid back in the
centre of the wall – back and back – until a
strange-shaped opening, about the size of the
train itself, showed in the thick wall. George
gasped. What was happening?

A man came through the opening. George felt
sure she'd seen him before somewhere. He came
up to the engine of the train and swung himself
into the driver's cab.

There were all sorts of sounds then from the
cab. What was the man doing? Starting the fire to
run the train? George didn't dare to try and see.
She was trembling now, and Timmy pressed
himself against her to comfort her.

Then came another set of noises – steam noises.
The man must be about to start the engine moving.
Smoke came from the funnel. More noises, and

some clanks and clangs.

It suddenly occurred to George that the man might be going to take the train through that little opening in the bricked-up wall. What if he closed the wall up again – George would be a prisoner! She'd be in the truck, hidden behind that wall, and the wall would be closed so that she couldn't escape.

'I have to get out before it's too late,' thought George, in a panic. 'I just hope the man doesn't see me!'

But just as she was about to try and get out, the engine gave a loud 'choo-choo', and began to move backwards! It ran down the lines a little way, then forward again, and this time its wheels were on the set of lines that led to the second tunnel, where the small opening now showed so clearly in the wall.

George didn't dare to get out of the moving train. So there she crouched as the engine steamed quickly to the hole in the wall that stretched right across the other tunnel. That hole just fitted it!

'It must have been made for it,' thought George, as the train moved through it.

The train went right through and came out in

another tunnel. Here there was a bright light, too. George peered out through the crack. There was more than a tunnel here! What looked like vast caves stretched away on each side of the tunnel, and men lounged about in them. Who on earth were they, and what were they doing with that old train?

There was a strange noise at the back of the train. The hole in the stout brick wall closed up once more! Now there was no way in or out.

'It's like the Open-Sesame trick in *Ali Baba and the Forty Thieves*,' thought George. 'And, like Ali Baba, I'm in the cave – and don't know the way to get myself out! I'm glad Timmy is with me!'

The train was now at a standstill. Behind it was the thick wall – and then George saw that in front of it was a thick wall, too! This tunnel must be bricked up in two places – and in between was this extraordinary cavern, or whatever it was. George couldn't understand it.

'What would the others say if they knew you and I were actually *in* the spook-train, tucked away in its hiding place where nobody in the world can find it?' whispered George to Timmy. 'What are we going to do, Timmy?'

Timmy wagged his tail cautiously. He didn't understand all this. He wanted to lie low for a bit and see how things turned out.

'We'll wait till the men have gone away, Timmy,' whispered George. 'That's if they ever do! Then we'll get out and see if we can manage that Open-Sesame entrance and get away. We'd better tell Mr Luffy about all this. There's something very strange and mysterious here – and we've fallen right into it!'

16 *In the tunnel again*

Jock was really enjoying himself at the camp. He had a picnic lunch with the others, and ate as much as they did, looking very happy. Mr Luffy joined them, and Jock beamed at him, feeling that he was a real friend.

'Where's George?' asked Mr Luffy.

'Gone off by herself,' said Julian.

'Have you argued, by any chance?' said Mr Luffy.

'A bit,' said Julian. 'We have to let George get over it by herself, Mr Luffy. She's like that.'

'Where's she gone?' said Mr Luffy, helping himself to a tomato. 'Why isn't she back for lunch?'

'She's taken hers with her,' said Anne. 'I feel a bit worried about her, somehow. I hope she's all right.'

Mr Luffy looked alarmed.

'I feel a bit worried myself,' he said. 'Still, she's got Timmy with her.'

'We're going off to do a bit of exploring,' said Julian, when they'd all finished eating. 'What are *you* going to do, Mr Luffy?'

'I think I'll come with you,' said Mr Luffy, unexpectedly.

The children's hearts sank. They couldn't possibly go exploring for spook-trains in the tunnel if Mr Luffy was with them.

'Well – I don't think it'll be very interesting for you, sir,' said Julian, rather feebly.

Mr Luffy took the hint and realised he wasn't wanted that afternoon.

'Right,' he said. 'In that case I'll stay here and mess about.'

The children sighed with relief. They cleared up and then they called goodbye to Mr Luffy and set off, taking their tea with them.

Jock was full of excitement. He was so pleased to be with the others, and he kept thinking of sleeping in the camp that night – it'd be fun! Good old Mr Luffy, taking his side like that. He bounded after the others joyfully as they went off to the old railway yard.

Wooden-Leg Sam was pottering about there as usual. They waved to him, but he didn't wave back. Instead he shook his fist at them and tried to bawl in his husky voice: 'You clear out! Trespassing, that's what you are. Don't you come down here or I'll chase you!'

'Well, we won't go down then,' said Dick, with a grin. 'We'll just walk along here, climb down the lines and walk up them to the tunnel.'

Which is what they did, much to the rage of poor Sam. He yelled till his voice gave out, but they took no notice, and walked quickly up the lines. The mouth of the tunnel looked very round and black as they came near.

'Now we'll walk right through this tunnel and see where that spook-train is,' said Julian. 'It didn't come out the other end, so it must be somewhere in the middle of the tunnel.'

'If it's a real spook-train, it might completely disappear,' said Anne, not liking the look of the dark tunnel.

The others laughed.

'It won't have disappeared,' said Dick. 'We'll find it somewhere, and we'll examine it and try and find out exactly what it is, and why it comes and goes in such a strange way.'

They walked into the black tunnel, and switched

on their torches, which made little gleaming paths in front of them. They walked up the middle of one pair of lines, Julian in front keeping a sharp lookout for anything in the shape of a train!

The lines ran on and on. The children's voices sounded strange and echoing in the long tunnel. Anne kept close to Dick, and half wished she hadn't come. Then she remembered that George had called her a coward, and she put up her head, determined not to show that she was scared.

Jock talked almost without stopping. 'I've never done anything like this in my life. This is a proper adventure, hunting for spook-trains in a dark tunnel. It makes me feel nice and shivery all over. I hope we find the train. It *must* be here somewhere!'

They walked on and on and on. But there was no sign of any train. They came to where the tunnel forked into the second one that used to run to Roker's Vale. Julian flashed his torch on the enormous brick wall that stretched across the second tunnel.

'Yes, it's well and truly bricked up,' he said. 'So that only leaves this tunnel to explore. Come on.'

They went on again, not knowing that George and Timmy were behind that brick wall, hidden in a truck of the spook-train itself! They walked on and on down the lines, and found nothing interesting at all.

They saw a little round circle of bright light some way in front of them.

'See that?' said Julian. 'That must be the end of this tunnel – the opening that goes into Kilty's Yard. Well, if the train isn't between here and Kilty's Yard, it's gone!'

In silence they walked down the rest of the tunnel, and came out into the open air. Workshops were built all over Kilty's Yard. The entrance to the tunnel was weed-grown and neglected. Weeds even grew across the lines there.

'No train has been out of this tunnel for years,' said Julian, looking at the thick weeds. 'The wheels would have chopped the weeds to bits.'

'It's so strange,' said Dick, puzzled. 'We've been right through the tunnel and there's no train there at all, yet we know it goes in and out of it. What's happened to it?'

'It is a spook-train,' said Jock, his face red with excitement. 'Must be. It only exists at night, and then comes out on its lines, like it used to do years ago.'

'I don't like thinking that,' said Anne, troubled. 'It's a horrible thought.'

'What are we going to do now?' Julian asked. 'We've drawn a blank. No train, nothing to see, empty tunnel. What a boring end to an adventure.'

'Let's walk back all the way again,' said Jock – he wanted to squeeze as much out of this adventure as he could. 'I know we won't see the train, but you never know!'

'I'm not going through that tunnel again,' said Anne. 'I want to be out in the sun. I'll walk over the top of the tunnel, along the path that Julian took the other night, and you three can walk back and meet me at the other end.'

'Right,' said Julian and the three boys disappeared into the dark tunnel.

Anne ran up the path that led alongside the top of it. It was good to be in the open air again! That horrible tunnel! She ran along cheerfully, glad to be out in the sun.

She got to the other end of the tunnel quite quickly, and sat down on the path above the yard to wait for the others. She looked for Wooden-

Leg Sam. He was nowhere to be seen. Perhaps he was in his little hut.

She hadn't been there for more than two minutes when something surprising happened. A car came bumping slowly down the rough track to the yard! Anne sat up and watched. A man got out – and Anne's eyes almost fell out of her head. It was Mr Andrews, Jock's stepfather!

He went over to Sam's hut and threw open the door. Anne could hear the sound of voices. Then she heard another noise – the sound of a heavy lorry coming. She saw it come cautiously down the steep, rough track. It ran into an old tumbledown shed and stayed there. Then three men came out and Anne stared at them. Where had she seen them before?

'Of course! They're the farm workers at Jock's farm!' she thought. 'But what are they doing here? How strange!'

Mr Andrews joined the men and, to Anne's alarm, they began to walk up the lines to the tunnel! Her heart almost stopped. Julian, Dick and Jock were still in that tunnel, walking through it. They would bump right into Mr Andrews and his men – and then what would happen? Mr

Andrews had warned them against going there, and had ordered Jock not to go.

Anne stared at the four men walking into the far-off mouth of the tunnel. What could she do? How could she warn the boys? She couldn't! She'd just have to stay there and wait for them to come out – probably chased by a furious Mr Andrews and the other men. If they were caught they'd probably all get a terrible telling off! What *could* she do?

'I can only wait,' thought poor Anne. 'There's nothing else to do. Oh, hurry up, Julian, Dick and Jock. I daren't do anything but wait for you.'

She waited and waited. It was now long past tea-time. Julian had the tea, so there was nothing for Anne to eat. Nobody came out of the tunnel. Not a sound was heard. Anne decided to go down and ask Wooden-Leg Sam a few questions. Feeling scared, the girl set off down to the yard.

Sam was in his hut, drinking hot chocolate, and looking very cross. Something had obviously gone wrong. When he saw Anne's shadow across the doorway he got up at once, shaking his fist.

'What, you children again! You went into that tunnel this afternoon, so I phoned Mr Andrews to come and catch you all, poking your noses in all the time. How did you get out of that tunnel? Are the others with you? Didn't Mr Andrews catch you?'

Anne listened to all this in horror. Sam had actually phoned Mr Andrews and told tales on them – so Jock's stepfather and his men had come to catch them. This was worse than ever.

'You come in here,' said Sam suddenly, and he reached his big arm out to her. 'Come on. I don't know where the others are, but I'll get one of you!'

Anne gave a scream and ran away at top speed. Wooden-Leg Sam went after her for a few yards and then gave up. He bent down and picked up a handful of earth. A shower of it fell all around Anne, and made her run faster than ever.

She raced up the path to the heather, and was soon on the moors again, panting and sobbing. 'Oh, Julian! Oh, Dick! What's happened to you? Oh, where's George? If only she'd come home, she'd be brave enough to look for them, but I'm not. I have to tell Mr Luffy. He'll know what to do!'

She ran on and on, her feet catching continually in the tufts of thick heather. She kept falling over and scrambling up again. She now had only one idea in her mind – to find Mr Luffy and tell him every single thing! Yes, she'd tell him about the spook-trains and all. There was something strange and important about the whole thing now, and she wanted a grown-up's help.

She staggered on and on. 'Mr Luffy! Oh, Mr Luffy, where are you? MR LUFFY!'

But no Mr Luffy answered her. She came around the gorse bushes she thought were the ones sheltering the camp – but the camp wasn't there. Anne had lost her way!

'I'm lost,' said Anne, the tears running down her cheeks. 'But I mustn't get scared. I have to try to find the right path now. But I'm completely lost! Mr LUFFY!'

Poor Anne. She stumbled on blindly, hoping to come to the camp, calling every now and again. 'Mr Luffy. Can you hear me? MR LUFFFFFFFY!'

17 An amazing find

In the meantime, what had happened to the three boys walking back through the tunnel? They'd gone slowly along examining the lines to see if a train could have possibly run along them recently. Few weeds grew in the dark airless tunnel, so they couldn't tell by those.

But, when they got about halfway, Julian noticed something interesting.

'Look,' he said, flashing his torch on to the lines behind and in front of them. 'See that? The lines are black and rusty behind us now, but here this pair of lines is quite shiny – as if they'd been used a lot.'

He was right. Behind them stretched black and rusty lines, sometimes buckled in places – but in front of them, stretching to the mouth of the tunnel leading to Olly's Yard, the lines were bright, as if train wheels had run along them.

'That's funny,' said Dick. 'Looks as if the spook-train ran only from here to Olly's Yard and back. But why? And where is it now? It's vanished into thin air!'

Julian was as puzzled as Dick. Where *could* a train be if it wasn't in the tunnel? It had obviously run to the middle of the tunnel, and then stopped – but where had it gone?

'Let's go to the mouth of the tunnel and see if the lines are bright all the way,' said Julian at last. 'We can't discover much here – unless the train suddenly materialises in front of us!'

They went on down the tunnel, their torches flashing on the lines in front of them. They didn't see four men waiting for them, four men who crouched in a little niche at the side of the tunnel, waiting in the dark.

'Well,' said Julian, 'I think—' and then he stopped, because four dark figures suddenly pounced on the three boys and held them tight. Julian gave a shout and struggled, but the man who had hold of him was far too strong to escape from. Their torches were flung to the ground. Julian's broke, and the other two torches lay there, their beams shining on the feet of the struggling company.

It didn't take more than twenty seconds to make each boy a prisoner, his arms behind his back. Julian tried to kick, but his captor twisted his arm so fiercely that he groaned in pain and stopped his kicking.

'What's all this about?' demanded Dick. 'Who are you, and what do you think you're doing? We're only three boys exploring an old tunnel. What's the harm in that?'

'Take them all away,' said a voice that everyone recognised at once.

'Mr Andrews! Is that you?' cried Julian. 'Let us go. You know us – the boys at the camp. And Jock's here too. What do you think you're doing?'

Mr Andrews didn't answer, but he gave poor Jock a shake that almost knocked him to the ground.

Their captors turned them around and led them roughly up the tunnel, towards the middle. Nobody had a torch so it was all done in the darkness and the three boys stumbled badly, though the men seemed sure-footed enough.

They came to a halt after a while. Mr Andrews left them and Julian heard him go off somewhere to the left. Then there was a strange noise – a bang, a clank, and then a sliding, grating sound. What was happening? Julian strained his eyes in the darkness, but he could see nothing at all.

He didn't know that Mr Andrews was opening the bricked-up wall through which the train had gone. He didn't know that he and the others were being pushed out of the first tunnel into the other one, through the strange hole in the wall. The three boys were shoved along in the darkness, not daring to protest.

Now they were in the secret place between the two walls – the place where the spook-train stood in silence – the place where George was, still hidden in one of the trucks with Timmy! But nobody knew that, of course; not even Mr Andrews guessed that a girl and a dog were listening in a truck nearby!

He put on a torch and flashed it in the faces of the three boys, who felt scared, although they weren't showing any fear. This was so strange and unexpected, and they had no idea where they were.

'You were warned not to go down to that yard,' said the voice of one of the men. 'You were told it was a bad and dangerous place. It is. And you've got to suffer for not listening to the warning! You'll be tied up and left here till we've finished our business. Maybe that'll be three days, maybe it'll be three weeks!'

'You can't keep us prisoners for all that time!' said Julian, alarmed. 'There'll be search parties out for us all over the place! They'll be sure to find us.'

'Oh, no they won't,' said the voice. 'Nobody will find you here. Now, Peters – tie 'em up!'

Peters tied the three boys up. They had their legs tied, and their arms too, and were pushed down roughly against a wall. Julian protested again.

'What are you doing this for? We're harmless. We don't know anything about your business, whatever it is.'

'We're not taking any chances,' said the voice. It wasn't Mr Andrews's voice, but a firm, strong one, full of determination and a large amount of annoyance.

'What about Mum?' said Jock suddenly, to his stepfather. 'She'll be worried.'

'Well, let her be worried,' said the voice again,

answering before Mr Andrews could say a word.
'It's your own fault. You were warned.'

The feet of the four men moved away. Then
there came the same noises again as the boys had
heard before. They were made by the hole in the
wall closing up, but the boys didn't know that.
They couldn't imagine what they were. The noises
stopped and there was dead silence. There was
also absolute darkness. The three boys strained
their ears, and felt sure that the men had gone.

'Those thugs! What are they up to?' said Julian
in a low voice, trying to loosen the ropes around
his hands.

'They've got a secret to hide,' said Dick.
'They've tied my feet so tightly that the rope is
cutting into my flesh.'

'What's going to happen?' came Jock's
scared voice.

This adventure didn't seem quite so exciting to
him now.

'Shh!' said Julian suddenly. 'I can hear
something!'

They all lay and listened. What was it they
could hear?

'It's – it's a dog whining,' said Dick, suddenly.

It was. It was Timmy in the truck with George. He'd heard the voices of the boys he knew, and he wanted to get to them. But George, not sure yet that the men had gone, still had her hand on his collar. Her heart thumped for joy to think she was no longer alone. The three boys – and Anne, too, perhaps – were there, in the same strange place as she and Timmy were.

The boys listened hard. The whining came again. Then George let go of Timmy's collar, and he leapt headlong out of the truck. His feet pattered eagerly over the ground. He went straight to the boys in the darkness, and Julian felt a wet tongue licking his face. A warm body pressed against him, and a little bark told him who it was.

'Timmy! Dick – it's Timmy!' cried Julian, in joy. 'Where did he come from? Timmy, is it really you?'

'Woof,' said Timmy, and licked Dick next and then Jock.

'Where's George then?' wondered Dick.

'Here,' said a voice, and out of the truck scrambled George, switching on her torch as she did so. She went over to the boys. 'What's happened? How did you get here? Were you captured or something?'

'Yes,' said Julian. 'But, George – where are we? And what are *you* doing here? It's like a strange dream!'

'I'll cut your ropes first, before I explain anything,' said George, and she took out her sharp penknife.

In a few moments she'd cut the boys' ropes, and they all sat up, rubbing their sore ankles and wrists, groaning.

'Thanks, George! I'm fine,' said Julian, getting up. 'Where *are* we? Hey, is that an engine there? What's it doing here?'

'That, Julian, is the spook-train!' said George, with a laugh. 'It is, honestly.'

'But we walked all the way down the tunnel and out of the other end, without finding it,' said Julian puzzled.

'Listen, Ju,' said George. 'You know where that second tunnel is bricked up, don't you? Well, there's a way in through the wall – a whole bit of it moves back in a sort of Open-Sesame way! The spook-train can run in through the hole, on the rails. Once it's beyond the wall it stops, and the hole is closed up again.'

George shone her torch around to show the astonished boys the wall through which they'd come. Then she swung her torch to the big wall opposite. 'See that?' she said. 'There are *two* walls across this second tunnel, with a big space in between – where the spook-train hides! Clever, isn't it?'

'It would be, if I could see any sense in it,' said Julian. 'But I can't. Why would anyone mess about with a silly spook-train at night?'

'That's what we've got to find out,' said George. 'And now's our chance. Look, Julian – look at all the caves stretching out on either side of the tunnel here. They would make wonderful hiding places!'

'What for?' said Dick. 'I don't get any of this!'

George swung her torch on the three boys and then asked a sudden question: 'Hey – where's Anne?'

'Anne! She didn't want to come back with us through the tunnel, so she ran over the moorlands to meet us at the other end, by Olly's Yard,' said Julian. 'She'll be worried sick, won't she, when we don't turn up? I hope she doesn't come wandering up the tunnel to meet us – she'll run into those men if she does.'

Everyone felt worried. Anne hated the tunnel and she'd be very frightened if people pounced on her in the darkness. Julian turned to George.

'Swing your torch around and let's see these caves. There doesn't seem to be anyone here now. We could have a look around.'

George swung her torch around, and Julian saw vast and apparently endless caves stretching out on either side, cut out of the sides of the tunnel. Jock saw something else. By the light of the torch he caught sight of a switch on the wall. Perhaps it opened the hole in the wall.

He crossed to it and pulled it down. Immediately the place was flooded with a bright light. It was a light-switch he'd found. They all blinked in the sudden glare.

'That's better,' said Julian, pleased. 'Well done, Jock! Now we can see what we're doing.'

He looked at the spook-train standing silently near them on its rails. It looked very old and forgotten – as if it belonged to the last century.

'It's a museum piece,' said Julian, with interest. 'So that's what we heard puffing in and out of the tunnel at night – old Spooky!'

'I hid in that truck there,' said George, pointing, and she told them her own adventure.

The boys could hardly believe she'd actually puffed into this secret place, hidden on the spook-train itself!

'Come on – let's look at these caves,' said Dick.

They went over to the nearest one. It was packed with crates and boxes of all kinds. Julian pulled one open and whistled.

'All black market stuff, I bet. Look – crates of whisky and brandy, boxes and boxes of stuff – who knows what! This is a real black-market hiding place!'

The boys explored a little further. The caves were piled high with valuable stuff, worth thousands of pounds.

'All stolen, I suppose,' said Dick. 'But what do they *do* with it? I mean – they bring it here in the train, of course, and hide it – but they must have some way of getting rid of it.'

'Would they repack it on the train and run it back to the yard when they had enough lorries to take it away?' said Julian.

'No!' said Dick. 'Of course not. Let me think

– they steal it, pile it on to lorries at night, take it somewhere temporarily . . .'

'Yes – to my mum's farm!' said Jock, in a scared voice. 'All those lorries there in the barn – that's what they're used for! And they come down to Olly's Yard at night and the stuff is loaded in secret on the old train that comes puffing out to meet them – and then it's taken back here and hidden!'

Julian whistled. 'You're right, Jock! That's exactly what happens. They use an honest little farm as a hiding place, fill the farm with black-market men – no wonder they're such bad workers – and they wait for dark nights to run the stuff down to the yard and load it on the train!'

'Your stepfather must make a lot of money doing this,' said Dick to Jock.

'Yes. That's why he can afford to pour money into the farm,' said Jock, miserably. 'Poor Mum. This'll break her heart. Still, I don't think my stepfather's the chief one in this. There's somebody else behind it.'

'Yes,' said Julian, thinking of the mean little Mr Andrews, with his big nose and weak chin. 'There probably is. Listen, I've thought of something else. If this stuff is got rid of in any other way except down the tunnel it came up, there must be another way out of these caves!'

'I think you're right,' said George. 'And if there is – we'll find it and escape that way!'

'Come on!' said Julian, and he switched off the glaring light. 'Your torch will give enough light now. We'll try this cave first. Keep your eyes open, all of you!'

18 A way of escape

The four children and Timmy went into the big cave. They made their way around piles of boxes, chests and crates, amazed at the amount the men must have stolen.

'These aren't man-made caves,' said Julian. 'They're natural. I expect the roof fell in where the two tunnels met, and the entrance between them was actually blocked up.'

'But were *two* walls built then?' said Dick.

'No. Who knows how this black-market hiding place came about,' said Julian, 'Perhaps people knew that there were caves here – and when someone came exploring along the tunnel one day, maybe they even found an old train buried under rubble or something like that.'

'And resurrected it, and built another wall secretly for a hiding place – and used the train for their own purposes!' said Dick. 'Made that secret entrance, too. Clever!'

They'd explored a lot of the cave by now, without finding anything of interest beyond the boxes, crates and chests. Then they came to a pile that was very neatly arranged, with numbers chalked on boxes that were built up one on top of another. Julian stopped.

'It looks as if these boxes are about to be shifted off somewhere,' he said. 'All put in order and numbered. Surely the exit must be somewhere here?'

He took George's torch from her and flashed it all around. Then he found what he wanted. The beam of light shone steadily on a strong, roughly made wooden door, set in the wall of the cave. They went over to it in excitement.

'This is what we want!' said Julian. 'I bet this is the exit to some very lonely part of the moors, not far from a road that lorries can come along to collect any goods carried out of here! There are some really deserted roads over these moors, running in the middle of miles of lonely moorland.'

'It's a clever organisation,' said Dick. 'Lorries stored at an innocent farm, full of goods for hiding in the tunnel-caves at a convenient time.

The train comes out in the dark to collect the goods, and takes them back here, till the police stop searching for them. Then they go out through this door to the moorlands, down to the lorries which come to collect them and whisk them away to the black market!'

'I told you how I saw Peters late one night, locking up the barn, didn't I?' said Jock, excitedly. 'He must have had the lorry full of stolen goods then – and the next night he loaded them on to the spook-train!'

'Exactly,' said Julian, who had been trying the door to see if he could open it. 'This door's stuck. I can't make it budge. There's no lock that I can see.'

They all shoved hard, but the door wouldn't give. It was very stout and strong, though rough and unfinished. Panting and hot, the four of them at last gave up.

'Do you know what I think?' said Dick. 'I think there's something jammed hard against it on the other side.'

'Yes, it must have, when you think about it,' said Julian. 'It'll be well hidden too – heather and bracken and stuff all over it. Nobody would ever find it. I suppose the lorry-drivers come across from the road to open the door when they want to collect the goods. And shut it and jam it after them.'

'No way of escape there, then,' said George in disappointment.

''Fraid not,' said Julian.

George gave a sigh.

'Tired?' Julian asked kindly. 'Or hungry?'

'Both,' said George.

'We've got some food somewhere, haven't we?' said Julian. 'I remember one of the men slinging my bag in after me. We haven't had what we brought for tea yet. How about having a meal now? We can't seem to escape at the moment.'

'Let's have it here,' said George. 'I can't go a step further!'

They sat down against a big crate. Dick undid his rucksack. There were sandwiches, cake and chocolate. The four of them ate thankfully, and wished they had something to wash down the food with. Julian kept wondering about Anne.

'I wonder what she did,' he said. 'She'd wait and wait, I suppose. Then she might go back to the camp. But she doesn't know the way very well, and she might get lost. I don't know which would be worse for Anne, being lost on the moor or a prisoner down here with us!'

'Perhaps she's neither,' said Jock, giving Timmy his last bit of sandwich. 'I'm really glad to have Timmy. Honestly, George, I couldn't believe it when I heard Tim whine, and then heard your voice, too. I thought I must be dreaming.'

They sat where they were for a little longer and then decided to go back to the tunnel where the train was.

'We might be able to find the switch that works the Open-Sesame bit,' said Julian. 'We ought to have looked before, really, but I didn't think of it.'

They went back to where the train stood silently on its pair of lines. It seemed such an ordinary old train now that the children couldn't imagine why they'd ever thought it was strange and spooky.

They switched on the light again, then they looked about for any lever or handle that might open the hole in the wall. There didn't seem to be anything at all. They tried a few switches, but nothing happened.

Then George suddenly came across a big lever

low down in the brick wall itself. She tried to move it and couldn't. She called Julian.

'Ju! Come here. I wonder if this has got anything to do with opening that hole.'

The three boys came over to George. Julian tried to swing the lever down. Nothing happened. He pulled it but it wouldn't move. Then he and Dick pushed it upwards with all their strength.

And hey presto, there came a bang from somewhere, as something heavy shifted, and then a clanking as if machinery was at work. Then came the sliding, grating noise and a big piece of the brick wall moved slowly back, and then swung around sideways and stopped. The way of escape was open!

'Open Sesame!' said Dick, grandly, as the hole appeared.

'Better switch off the light here,' said Julian. 'If there's anyone still in the tunnel they might see the reflection of it on the tunnel-wall, and wonder what it was.'

He stepped back and switched it off, and the place was in darkness again. George put on her torch, and its feeble beam lit up the way of escape.

'Come on,' said Dick, impatiently, and they

all crowded out of the hole. 'Let's head for Olly's Yard.'

They began to make their way down the dark tunnel.

'Listen,' said Julian, in a low voice. 'We'd better not talk at all, and we'd better go as quietly as we can. We don't know who may be in or out of this tunnel this evening. We don't want to walk into somebody.'

So they said nothing at all, but kept close to one another in single file, walking at the side of the track.

They hadn't gone far when Julian stopped suddenly. The others bumped into one another, and Timmy gave a little whine as somebody trod on his paw. George's hand went down to his collar at once.

The four of them and Timmy listened, hardly daring to breathe. Somebody was coming up the tunnel towards them! They could see the pinpoint of a torch, and hear the distant crunch of footsteps.

'Other way, quick!' whispered Julian, and they all turned. With Jock leading them now, they made their way as quickly and quietly as they could back to the place where the two tunnels met. They passed it and went on towards Kilty's Yard, hoping to get out that way.

But a light was shining some way down the tunnel there, and they didn't dare to go on. There might be nobody with the light – on the other hand there might. What were they going to do?

'They'll see that hole in the wall is open!' said Dick suddenly. 'We left it open. They'll know we've escaped. We'll be caught again! They'll come down to find us, and here we'll be!'

They stood still, pressed close together, Timmy growling a little in his throat. Then George remembered something!

'Julian! Dick! We could climb up that vent that I came down,' she whispered. 'The one Timmy fell down. Have we got time?'

'Where's the vent?' said Julian, urgently. 'Quick, find it.'

George tried to remember. Yes, it was on the other side of the tunnel – near the place where the two tunnels met. She must look for the pile of soot. She hoped the little light from her torch wouldn't be seen. Whoever was coming up from Olly's Yard must be almost there by now!

She found the pile of soot that Timmy had fallen into.

'Here it is,' she whispered. 'Julian! How can we take Timmy?'

'We can't,' said Julian. 'We just have to hope he'll manage to hide and then slink out of the tunnel by himself. He's clever enough.'

He pushed George up the vent first and her feet found the first rungs. Then Jock went up, his nose almost on George's heels. Then Dick – and last of all, Julian. But before he managed to climb the first steps, something happened.

A bright glare filled the tunnel, as someone switched on the light that hung there. Timmy slunk into the shadows and growled in his throat. Then there was a shout.

'Who's opened the hole in the wall? It's open! Who's there?'

It was Mr Andrews's voice. Then came another voice, angry and loud: 'Who's here? Who's opened this place?'

'Those kids can't have moved the lever,' said Mr Andrews. 'We tied them up tightly.'

The men, three of them, went quickly through the hole in the wall. Julian climbed up the first few rungs thankfully. Poor Timmy was left in the shadows at the bottom.

Out came the men at a run. 'They've gone! Their ropes are cut! How could they have escaped? We put Kit down one end of the tunnel and we've been walking up this end. Those kids must be about here somewhere.'

'Or hiding in the caves,' said another voice. 'Peters, go and look, while we hunt here.'

The men hunted everywhere. They had no idea that the vent was nearby in the wall. They didn't see the dog that slunk by them like a shadow, keeping out of their way, and lying down whenever the light from a torch came near him.

George climbed steadily, feeling with her feet for the iron nails whenever she came to broken rungs. Then she came to a stop. Something was pressing on her head. What was it? She put up her hand to feel. It was the collection of broken iron bars that Timmy had fallen on that morning. He'd dislodged some of them, and they had fallen in such a way that they had lodged across the vent, all twined into each other. George could climb no higher. She tried to move the bars, but they were heavy and strong – besides, she was afraid she might bring the whole lot down on her and the others. They might be badly hurt.

'What's up, George? Why have you stopped?' asked Jock, who was next.

'There are some iron bars across the vent – ones that must have fallen when Timmy fell,' said George. 'I can't go any higher! I daren't pull too hard at the bars.'

Jock passed the message to Dick, and he passed it down to Julian. The four of them came to a full stop!

'Oh no!' said Julian. 'I wish I'd gone up first. What are we to do now?'

What indeed? The four of them hung there in the darkness, hating the smell of the sooty old vent, miserably uncomfortable on the broken rungs and nails.

'How do you like adventures now, Jock?' asked Dick. 'I bet you wish you were in your own bed at home!'

'I don't!' said Jock. 'I wouldn't miss this for worlds! I always wanted an adventure – and I'm not grumbling at this one!'

19 What an adventure!

Meanwhile, what had happened to Anne? She had stumbled on and on for a long time, shouting to Mr Luffy. And outside his tent Mr Luffy sat, reading peacefully. But, as the evening came, and then darkness, he became very worried indeed about the five children.

He wondered what to do. It was hopeless for one man to search the moors. Half a dozen or more were needed for that! He decided to get his car and go over to Olly's Farm to get the men from there. So off he went.

But when he got there he found no one at home except Mrs Andrews. Mrs Andrews looked bewildered and worried.

'What's the matter?' asked Mr Luffy gently, as she came running out to the car, looking troubled.

'Oh, it's you, Mr Luffy,' she said, when he told her who he was. 'I didn't know who you were.

Mr Luffy, something strange is happening. All the men have gone – and all the lorries, too. My husband has taken the car and nobody will tell me anything. I'm so worried.'

Mr Luffy decided not to add to her worries by telling her that the children were missing. He just pretended he'd come to collect some milk.

'Don't worry,' he said comfortingly to Mrs Andrews. 'You'll find things are all right in the morning, I expect. I'll come and see you then. Now I must be off on an urgent matter.'

He went bumping along the road in his car, puzzled. He'd known there was something funny about Olly's Farm, and he'd done a lot of thinking about Olly's Yard and the spook-trains. He hoped the children hadn't got mixed up in anything dangerous.

'I'd better go down and report to the police that they're missing,' he thought. 'After all, I'm more or less responsible for them. It's very worrying indeed.'

He told what he knew at the police station, and the sergeant, an intelligent man, at once mustered six officers and a police car.

'Have to find those kids,' he said. 'And we'll

have to look into this Olly's Farm business, sir, and these spook-trains, whatever they may be. We've known there was something funny going on, but we couldn't put our finger on it. But we'll find the children first.'

They went quickly up to the moors and the six men began to fan out to search, with Mr Luffy at the head. And the first thing they found was Anne!

She was still stumbling along, crying for Mr Luffy, but in a very small, weak voice now. When she heard his voice calling her in the darkness she wept for joy.

'Oh, Mr Luffy! You have to save the boys,' she begged him. 'They're in that tunnel – and I'm sure they've been caught by Mr Andrews and his men. They didn't come out and I waited and waited! Please come!'

'I've got some friends here who will certainly come and help,' said Mr Luffy gently. He called the policemen, and in a few words told them what Anne had said.

'In the tunnel?' said one of them. 'Where the spook-trains run? Come on, men, we'll go down there.'

'You stay behind, Anne,' said Mr Luffy.

But she wouldn't. So he carried her as he followed the policemen who were making their way through the heather, down to Olly's Yard. They didn't bother with Wooden-Leg Sam. They went straight to the tunnel and walked up it quietly. Mr Luffy was a good way behind with Anne. She refused to stay with him in the yard.

'No,' she said, 'I'm not a coward. Really I'm not. I want to help to rescue the boys. I wish George was here. Where's George?'

Mr Luffy had no idea. Anne clung to his hand, scared but eager to prove that she wasn't a coward. Mr Luffy thought she was very brave!

Meanwhile, Julian and the others had been in the vent for a long time, tired and uncomfortable. The men had searched in vain for them and were now looking closely into every niche at the sides of the tunnel.

And, of course, they found the vent! One of the men shone his light up it. It shone on to poor Julian's feet! The man gave a loud shout that almost made Julian fall off the rung he was standing on.

'Here they are! Up this vent. Who'd have thought it? Come on down or you'll be sorry!'

Julian didn't move. George pushed desperately at the iron bars above her head, but she couldn't move them. One of the men climbed up the vent and grabbed Julian's foot.

He dragged so hard at it that the boy's foot was forced off the rung. Then the man dragged off the other foot, and Julian found himself hanging by his arms with the man tugging hard at his feet. He could hang on no longer. His tired arms gave way and he fell heavily down, landing half on the man and half on the pile of soot. Another man pounced on Julian at once, while the first climbed up the vent to find the next boy. Soon Dick felt his feet being tugged at, too.

'All right, all right. I'll come down!' he yelled, and climbed down.

Then Jock climbed down, too. The men looked at them angrily.

'Giving us a chase like this! Who undid your ropes?' said Mr Andrews, roughly.

One of the men put a hand on his arm and nodded up towards the vent.

'Someone else is coming down,' he said. 'We

only tied up three boys, didn't we? Who's this, then?'

It was George, of course. She wasn't going to desert the three boys. Down she came, as black as night with soot.

'Another boy!' said the men. 'Where did he come from?'

'Any more up there?' asked Mr Andrews.

'Look and see,' said Julian, and got a smack on the head for his answer.

'Treat them rough,' ordered Peters. 'Teach them a lesson, the little pests. Take them away.'

The children's hearts sank. The men caught hold of them roughly. Now they would be made prisoners again.

Suddenly a cry came from down the tunnel: 'Police! Run for it!'

The men dropped the children's arms at once and stood undecided. A man came tearing up the tunnel.

'The police are coming!' he gasped. 'Are you stone deaf? There's a whole crowd of them. Run for it! Somebody's grassed on us.'

'Get along to Kilty's Yard!' shouted Peters. 'We can get cars there. Run for it!'

To the children's dismay, the men raced down the tunnel to Kilty's Yard. They would escape! They heard the sound of the men's feet as they ran along the line.

George found her voice. 'Timmy! Where are you? After them, Timmy! Stop them!'

A black shadow came streaking by out of the hole in the wall, where Timmy had been hiding and watching for a chance to come to George. He'd heard her voice and obeyed. He raced after the men like a greyhound, his tongue hanging out, panting as he went.

These were the men who had ill-treated George and the others, were they? Aha, Timmy knew how to deal with people like that!

The policemen came running up, and Mr Luffy and Anne came up behind them.

'They've gone down there, with Timmy after them,' shouted George.

The policemen looked at her and gasped. She was black all over. The others were filthy dirty too, with sooty faces in the light that shone down from the wall of the tunnel.

'George!' shrieked Anne in delight. 'Julian! Oh, are you all safe? I went back to tell Mr Luffy about you and I got lost. I'm so ashamed!'

'You've got nothing to be ashamed of, Anne,' said Mr Luffy. 'You're a wonderful girl! Brave as a lion!'

From down the tunnel came shouts and yells and loud barks. Timmy was at work! He'd caught up with the men and launched himself on them one after another, bringing each one heavily to the ground. They were terrified to find a big animal growling and snapping all around them. Timmy held them in the tunnel, not allowing them to go one step further, snapping at any man who dared to go near him.

The police ran up. Timmy growled extra fiercely just to let the men know that it was impossible to get past him. Soon each of the men was imprisoned by a pair of strong arms and they were being told to come quietly.

They didn't go quietly. Mr Andrews lost his nerve and cried. Jock felt very ashamed of him.

'Shut up,' said a burly policeman. 'We know you're only the miserable little cat's-paw – taking money from the big men to hold your tongue and obey orders.'

Timmy barked as if to say, 'Yes, don't you dare

call him a *dog's*-paw! That'd be too good a name for him!'

'I don't think I've ever seen dirtier children in my life,' said Mr Luffy. 'I suggest we all go back to my car and I drive the lot of you over to Olly's Farm for a meal and a bath!'

So back they all went, tired, dirty, and also feeling very excited.

What a night! They told Anne all that had happened, and she told them her story, too. She almost fell asleep in the car as she talked, she was so tired.

Mrs Andrews was sensible and kind, although very upset to hear that her husband had been taken off by the police. She got hot water for baths, and laid a meal for the hungry children.

'I wouldn't worry too much, Mrs Andrews,' said kindly Mr Luffy. 'That husband of yours needs a lesson. This will probably keep him going straight in future. The farm is yours, and now you can hire proper farm workers who'll do what you want them to do. And I think Jock will be happier without a stepfather for now.'

'You're right, Mr Luffy,' said Mrs Andrews, wiping her eyes quickly. 'Quite right. I'll let Jock help me with the farm, and keep it going. I can hardly believe that Mr Andrews was in with all those black marketeers! It's that friend of his, you know, who makes him do all this. He's so weak. He knew Jock was snooping about in that tunnel, and that's why he wanted him to go away. I knew there was something funny going on.'

'No wonder he was worried when Jock took it into his head to go and camp with our little lot,' said Mr Luffy.

'To think of that old yard and tunnel being used again!' said Mrs Andrews. 'And all those tales about spook-trains – and the way they hid that train, and hid all the stuff, too. It's like a fairy tale, isn't it!'

She went to see if the water was hot for the baths. It was, and she went to call the children, who were in the big bedroom next door. She opened it and looked in. Then she called Mr Luffy upstairs.

He looked in at the door, too. The five, and Timmy, were lying on the floor in a heap, waiting for their baths. They hadn't liked to sit on chairs or beds, they were so dirty. And they'd fallen asleep where they sat, their faces black with soot.

'Talk about black marketeers!' whispered Mrs Andrews. 'Anyone would think we'd got the whole lot of them here in the bedroom!'

They all woke up and went to have a bath one by one, and a good meal after that. Then back to camp with Mr Luffy, Jock with them, too.

It was glorious to snuggle down into the sleeping bags. George called out to the three boys.

'Now don't you dare to go off without me tonight!'

'The adventure's over,' called back Dick. 'How did you like it, Jock?'

'Like it?' said Jock, with a happy sigh. 'It was absolutely – fantastic!'

www.famousfivebooks.com

Check out the brand new Famous Five website.

Featuring games and downloads from avatars to
screen savers for mobile phones and wallpapers.
Enter our amazing monthly competitions and online
team challenges to win fab prizes, including
limited edition merchandise only available
on the website.

www.famousfivebooks.com
www.hodderchildrens.co.uk

THE
FAMOUS
FIVE ADVENTURE GAME BOOK

Meet the Famous Five and be part of the adventure in these bumper fun game books.

Follow the clues and solve the mystery but watch out for red herrings!

For more fun and games visit www.famousfivebooks.com

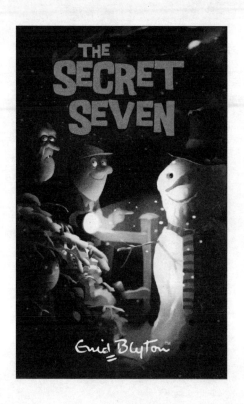

Meet Peter, Janet and Jack, Barbara, Pam, Colin and
George. Together they are The Secret Seven –
ready to solve any mystery, anytime!
A great introduction to adventure stories.

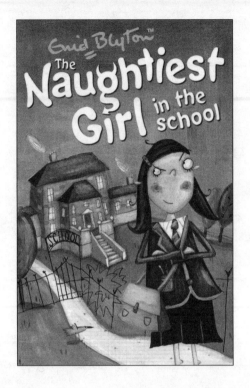

Elizabeth Allen is spoilt, mischievous and determined
to get home – whatever the cost – she really is the
Naughtiest Girl in the school! Exciting stories about
the girls and boys boarding at Whyteleafe School.